Cortlandt Parker

Philip Kearny

Soldier and Patriot

Cortlandt Parker

Philip Kearny
Soldier and Patriot

ISBN/EAN: 9783337307691

Printed in Europe, USA, Canada, Australia, Japan

Cover: Foto ©Raphael Reischuk / pixelio.de

More available books at **www.hansebooks.com**

PHILIP KEARNY:

SOLDIER AND PATRIOT.

AN ADDRESS

DELIVERED BEFORE THE

NEW-JERSEY HISTORICAL SOCIETY,

JANUARY 17, 1867,

BY

CORTLANDT PARKER.

PUBLISHED BY REQUEST.

NEWARK:

FROM THE "NORTHERN MONTHLY."

—

1868.

MAJOR-GENERAL PHILIP KEARNY.

THE task before me is a labor of love. Philip Kearny, as a soldier and a patriot: this is my theme—a fit one for the Historical Society of New-Jersey, for the favorites of history are patriots and soldiers. And Philip Kearny was both the splendid soldier and the ardent patriot; and, sprung from New-Jersey blood, nurtured on Jersey soil, leading to the field New-Jersey's first brigade, regarding himself through all the war for the Union as a Jersey soldier, it is fit and right—it is, in fact, our duty—to set forth, justly but fully, the splendid career of this martyr to our cause.

Philip Kearny was born June 2d, 1815. He was the son of Philip Kearny, of Newark, and his wife, Susan Watts, daughter of John Watts, of New-York, founder of the Leake and Watts Orphan Asylum there, and distinguished for wealth and generosity. Through his father his lineage was Irish, and it is not difficult to discern that many salient points of his character were derived from that impulsive, generous, brave, and danger-loving blood. His mother was descended, in part, from Huguenot ancestry. Her lineage was of the De Lanceys, and it is said that both in appearance and character her son very much resembled this branch of his ancestry. They were soldiers by nature. The name is distinguished in the history of chivalry. And nothing can be more striking than the similarity in personal appearance between the subject of this sketch, and at least one of his near relatives on the mother's side, whose face and form are said to be that of the De Lancey family.

General Kearny's father resided in Newark. The simple, reverend-looking old mansion of the family still stands, shaded by magnificent old elms in the environs of that growing city, and as yet in possession of the family, who retain its quaint peculiarities with pious care. But Mrs. Kearny's friends lived in New-York. She often visited them, and during her temporary residence there this her only son was born. But he was nurtured from early childhood in Newark, went to school there, regarded that as his home, established his own costly residence near it, and was to all intents and purposes a Jerseyman.

I have been able to learn little of his childhood and youth. His schoolmates speak of him as a delicate boy, averse to violent sports, and holding himself somewhat aloof from promiscuous companionship. He was not a student, nor apparently in anywise ambitious of distinction.

One relative, himself an enthusiast in military literature, represents him as having always had the greatest interest in those matters. Together, he says, they studied the battles of great captains, and with mimic soldiers fought them over again; addressing themselves with industry to master the details of the engagements of Cæsar Marlborough, and Napoleon, and, with maps and models before them, repeating the strategic moves upon which the fate of nations so often hung.

Young Kearny soon pursued the natural bent of his genius. In obedience to the wishes of his father and friends, he passed regularly through Columbia College; then studied law. But, as soon as he had arrived at majority, he abandoned studies which, it is easy to see, must have been very irksome to such a nature, obtained a commission in a regiment of dragoons, which, with others, his uncle, General Stephen W. Kearny, had aided in organizing, and immediately went with it to join that distinguished officer in the West.

This was in 1837. He spent something over a year on this service, meantime devoting himself with great ardor to the details of the military profession, and acquiring skill in horsemanship.

A singular circumstance may be interesting here. Jefferson Davis was captain in the same regiment of dragoons at the time that Philip Kearny was lieutenant! How widely divergent their subsequent paths of life and thought!

In the year 1839, the French government accorded to the United States permission to send three officers to follow the course of instruction in their military school at Saumur. Our Government selected Lieutenant Kearny as one of them. He went there in 1840. These three youths made good use of their time, and among other things made a translation for our Government of French military tactics, the same afterward translated by Hardee. After a while Kearny left the school to go with the French forces to Africa. He was attached to the first Chasseurs d'Afrique, (Colonel Guie, under General Pays de Bourjolly,) and was present at at least two engagements, the taking of Millionat and the second battle of the Col di Yeveah. On this service he was greatly admired for his dash, skill, and fearlessness, and acquired the highest esteem of his colonel, who, in later days, followed his career with the warmest interest and pride. Many anecdotes are told of his gallantry in this war, of which his splendid horsemanship made him a hero. An American relative,

already alluded to as resembling him, when long afterward in
Algiers, was accosted by French soldiers with earnest inquiries
respecting their old comrade, whom they described as charging the
Arab cavalry, his sword in one hand, his pistol in the other, while
he held his reins in his teeth.

Lieutenant Kearny returned from France in 1841, and was attached to the staff of General Scott, in whose military family he remained
till the outbreak of the war with Mexico. Having risen at that time
to be captain of dragoons, he went to the West, and principally in
Illinois recruited his company. He was determined that it should be
worth leading, and called to his aid his private fortune. He offered
a premium additional to government bounty, both for men and
horses. A rather eccentric but earnestly patriotic lawyer, resident
in Springfield, Illinois, Abraham Lincoln by name, took much interest in his plans and aided their execution. And when the young
captain took the field, it was at the head of one hundred men,
selected for their superiority as horsemen and their intelligence,
mounted each on an iron-gray charger, picked for speed and blood.
Such another troop the army did not possess. General Scott took it
as his body-guard. And, therefore, its leader burned in vain for
personal distinction through all Scott's magnificent campaign until
the battle of Churubusco, fought, it will be remembered, at the very
gates of Mexico. But it is evident that the position beside the
General-in-Chief must have tended to perfect the ambitious young
officer in military strategy.

At this battle of Churubusco, to prevent being outflanked, General
Scott had given up his escort, and retired upon his centre, having
first detached Captain Kearny for "general service." An opportunity soon offered for distinguished usefulness, his behavior in which
is thus described by General Harney in his report: "At this
moment, perceiving that the enemy were retreating in disorder on
one of the main causeways leading to the city, I collected all the
cavalry within my reach, consisting of Captain Ker's company of
Second Dragoons, Captain Kearny's company of First Dragoons, and
Captains McReynolds and Dupenc's companies of the Third Dragoons,
and pursued them vigorously until we were halted by the discharge
of batteries at the gate. Many of the enemy were overtaken in the
pursuit and cut down by our sabres. I can not speak in terms too
complimentary of the manner in which this charge was executed.
My only difficulty was to restrain the impetuosity of my men and
officers, who seemed to vie with each other who should be foremost
in this pursuit. Captain Kearny gallantly led his squadron into the
very intrenchments of the enemy, and had the misfortune to lose an
arm from a grape-shot fired at one of the main gates of the capital."

In General Scott's report it is said: "The cavalry charge was headed by Captain Kearny of the First Dragoons, having in squadron with his own troop that of Captain McReynolds of the Third, making the usual escort to headquarters; but being early in the day detached for general service was now under Colonel Harney's orders. The gallant Captain Kearny, not hearing the recall that had been sounded, dashed up to the San Antonio gate, sabring all who resisted."

I received from a party engaged a graphic account of this charge. Mexico is approached at the spot in question by a narrow causeway crossing a deep marsh, which flanks it on either side. The Mexicans, routed and affrighted, retreated over this causeway in great confusion, seeking the protection of the gates and of a battery which guarded them. It was evident to Kearny, after getting upon this causeway, when he discovered this battery, that his safety lay in remorselessly continuing the charge, giving the retreating force no time to breathe. If he stopped, they would open their ranks, retire to each side of the road, and then his command would be destroyed by the fire of the Mexican artillery. An officer of great distinction in the late civil war was sent to command his return. Kearny rapidly pointed out to him his situation, which was unknown at headquarters, and remonstrated against the direction given. "General Scott does not know, and can not see," was the hurried argument, "else he would wish no retreat." Convinced, the messenger withheld his orders, joined the charging column, and with Captain Kearny almost entered the gate itself. It was, it is said, as Captain Kearny was returning, that the enemy, regaining their senses, fired a volley of grape, which carried away his left arm.

For his gallantry on this occasion Captain Kearny was promoted to be major. In 1850–1852, he was employed in California and Oregon against the Indian tribes, and then, resigning his commission, traveled extensively throughout Europe and the East, making his residence in Paris. He returned to this country for a short time at various periods, but lived principally in that great metropolis thenceforward until the breaking out of the rebellion in this country.

In 1859, the Italian war occurred. Major Kearny lost no time in endeavoring to witness the art he so enthusiastically studied when practiced on so grand a scale; was attached as aid-de-camp to the staff of General Morris, commanding the cavalry of the guard, and was present, under fire, at the battle of Solferino. His faculties, long devoted to the study of the art of war with an earnestness few were aware of, had then ripened with age. He made every use of his opportunities, and acquired a professional instinct which was very remarkable, and attracted attention. In consideration of his services the Emperor Napoleon III. conferred on him the cross of the

Legion of Honor, a decoration the more valued by him because he alone of his nation received it for military services.

As soon as it was clear that the existence of the American nation was imperiled, and that war on this continent was imminent, Major Kearny broke up his luxurious establishment in Paris and hastened to tender his sword to his government. He arrived in this country early in the spring of 1861, applied to General Scott for employment, and, at his instance, sought a commission first from the governor of New-York.

There was much more patriotism in this conduct than a hasty consideration would perceive. It was not only a sacrifice of the luxuries and amenities which had become to him a second nature, and which his wealth enabled him so largely to enjoy. But he had been the intimate of most of the Southern military men. Beauregard, Ewell, Lee, Longstreet, Magruder, the Hills, and others had been his associates, some at Paris as well as in America. His style of life and thought was more like them than that of the cooler and quieter North. He wrote of himself, even after the war began, in a valuable letter concerning the blacks, to which we shall recur : "There is no more Southern man at heart than myself. I am so from education, association, and from being a purely unprejudiced lover of the Union." His immediate relations were dead. There were none North whom he so especially loved or who had such claims on him that he should leave his life of wealth and ease, cross the ocean and fight for them. Yet he did not hesitate a moment. " What am I," he exclaimed, " if no longer an American ?" There was the argument in a nut-shell—nationality; that was the cause for which he fought. Like the old Roman, wherever he went, his pride was in his citizenship. " I am an American citizen," was his boast, his defense, his pride. He loved his country, its grand present, its almost infinitely grander future. He saw the crumbling of foreign empires, the worthless trial of foreign greatness. He saw clearly how all that was old was destined to sure decay, and how much the world was to owe to the freedom, the education, the civilization of the American Republic. And then, too, America was his country. To her he had sworn allegiance. For her he had lost his arm ; for her he had braved death on every battle-field from Vera Cruz to Mexico, and at the hands of the treacherous savage. And so, to save the nation, to do his part to secure her existence, and put down the villainy and insanity which threatened her life, though dissuaded by all his military friends in Paris, he hastened to give all the energies of his nature to the cause of his dear country. Those who conversed with him and knew the thoughts of his heart, and those alone, can know how firm and unalloyed was the patriotism which brought him home.

He was not welcomed as he should have been. It took long to convince the North upon what a desperate struggle they were entering. Spite of Sumter, most thought the coming war little more than an exciting holiday. Even Lincoln seemingly imagined that seventy-five thousand men were enough for the crisis, and did not comprehend the meaning of the derisive laugh with which the conspirators at Montgomery received his call for them. And so, instead of looking everywhere for ability and capacity in order that they might be placed in command, crowds of insignificant and incapable holiday chieftains besieged the authorities, seeking, and in many cases actually obtaining it, while those who deserved it and could be useful served in minor stations.

And so Philip Kearny, after weeks of waiting at the doors of the New-York executive, jostled by political intriguers, turned away in perfect disgust, absolutely unable, since he could not be a private with one arm, to find a place where he could serve the country he had come three thousand miles to fight for.

Accident placed a Jersey friend in possession of the fact that he was in America. The noble first brigade of three years' troops was then gathering for the field from which so few of them returned. It was evident at a glance that all such men needed was a leader who could appreciate their merits. Without Major Kearny's knowledge, this friend hastened to urge his appointment to command them. It was a matter of much more difficulty than he imagined. Looking back, it seems inconceivable how it could have cost so much exertion to secure the appointment of such a man to such a place. It took nearly three months to accomplish it. Not until Bull Run had illustrated our need of educated, experienced soldiers was it done. And how, in the mean time, did the restless spirit of the patriot hero chafe at he delay—for he knew his own capacity and appreciated the character of the war. Sure that the nation would eventually triumph, he knew, then, nevertheless, that it was all which experience has found it to be.

When the news of Bull Run came, he at once proclaimed his willingness to lead a regiment, or even to take a subordinate line command in any which should be raised. But the good Lincoln, who had recognized the Captain *Kerney*, as he pronounced his name, whom he had known in Illinois while raising his famous troop, in the one-armed Major Kearny about whom so much had been said to him by friends and foes, hastened, after that terrible national disgrace, to surround himself with all worthy of command, and high upon his list of brigadiers placed the name of Philip Kearny.

Within twenty-four hours after notice of his appointment, he joined the troops at Alexandria. The Jersey brigade happened to be lying together. Therefore, in spite of a strong desire on the part of the then Secretary of War to separate them, in order to abolish State pride even in such a matter, he was able to procure himself to be assigned to their command, and entered upon his duties with constitutional alacrity.

Those who had most strongly urged the appointment of General Kearny had no expectation that he would possess such excellence as he immediately displayed. His dash, his chivalric bravery, his generosity and lavish expenditure of his large wealth to make his troops compare favorably with others—what Scott said of him in a letter commending his appointment, "His long and valuable experience in actual military service seems to commend him as a useful as well as available commander and disciplinarian; he is among the bravest of the brave, and of the highest military spirit and bearing"—such considerations as these induced his advocates to prefer him among the competitors for the brigadiership which was expected by New-Jersey. There was no idea of his talents as an organizer, his fervid enthusiasm for his profession, his close study of the art of war and intimate acquaintance with its history, his magnetic influence over men, his intuitive perception of character, his strategic genius, and his almost more than conscientious devotion to his military duty. But a single month revealed all of those qualities of which circumstances would present the exhibition. Personally and intimately acquainted myself with the leading officers of his finest regiment, I was astonished to find his first letter, written a week after knowing them, photograph their characters as if he had always been their companion. And he addressed himself with such energy to the improvement of his brigade that, in three months, it was confessedly the best disciplined around Washington. His severity, sometimes brusque, often eccentric, at first made him unpopular. But the men soon saw that he was less indulgent to the shortcomings of officers than to theirs; that he studied their comfort and aimed at their improvement. Both officers and men soon found that there was but one path to his good will, one way of escaping severity, the full and punctilious discharge of duty; and that, if they were equal to its requisitions, they were not only appreciated but most generously applauded, while any thing like shunning duty met with most terrible rebuke. And they saw that he required nothing but what he himself did; that his days and nights were spent fitting himself for greater duties, or carefully attending to their best interests. And so, soon, they came to love him, worship him. They would go with him anywhere, reposing, without question, on his judgment.

A private letter from an intelligent sergeant in his command, written and published while our brigade was in Alexandria, tells the story so well that we are tempted to reproduce it :

"As regards our General, I will endeavor to give you some of the traits of his character in connection with his command.   1st. He is untiring in his efforts to promote the comfort and well-being of his men.   For instance : I was standing the other day engaged in conversation with Dr. Suckley, the brigade-surgeon, who, by the way, is a first-rate man, having been in the U. S. service for the past fifteen years, when one of General Kearny's orderlies rode up and placed a small packet in his hand with the general's compliments.   The doctor opened it and found wrapped up in a note $25 in gold, the note saying it came from General Kearny for Dr. Suckley to use for luxuries for the patients in the hospital under his (Dr. Suckley's) charge.   'There,' said the doctor, 'that is fifty dollars he has sent me for that purpose since we have been here, some two months.'

"2d. His discipline is of the strictest kind ; though there is never any thing like domineering or arrogance about him, yet he will have his rules and the regulations carried out, as to drill, etc., to the very letter.

"The brigade is fast approaching what I should judge to be its legitimate and proper standard of military perfection, under his unceasing endeavors to make it what he says it shall be, if the officers and men will only bear a helping hand, namely, the most useful and efficient in the service.

"3d. When we came over into Virginia, the officers cared little, and of course the men cared less, about doing things by system, even than while we were stationed at Camp Olden, Trenton ; but under his guidance no person would believe that this was the same body of troops; perfect order about every thing, men look neater, and appear to better advantage on parades or reviews, and drill better. In fact there has been a complete revolution of everything appertaining to the whole brigade.

"4th. I can compare his popularity with the men to nothing else but to the French army in the days of Napoleon I. ; they almost worship him, and would follow wherever—follow did I say ? no, they would *go* wherever he points as the path of duty.

"5th. Their confidence in his military skill is unparalleled in the history of *this* country since the days of Washington.   He seems to have every little item of military education and stratagem necessary to be used in such a campaign as this at his fingers' ends, and, no matter what he may be doing, should any officer ask his opinion on this point, or his advice on that particular, he will give either just as if he had been thinking of nothing else than the subject suggested by the question ; in a word, he is a military man in the strictest sense of that term.   His perception of the capabilities of a man for any work he may be wanted for is as quick as lightning, and he only needs a glance.   He is also very strict about members of other brigades coming inside our lines without passes, and we have had orders to arrest any such found on the roads or in any of the camps, while we may be on patrol duty ; also any of our own men found outside *our* lines, without passes from their colonels.   You can judge, by these instances, somewhat of his character as a disciplinarian.

"I think I have written quite enough to convince any person of his fitness for the responsible post he now occupies.   The question used to be asked, before he came, 'Who shall lead us on ?' but now it is, 'When shall we be led to meet our enemies ?'   There are no fears of the result of such a meeting for an instant crossing our minds. Our final success is sure. Perhaps many will fall before it is attained. I may be of the number; but if I should, I wish all my friends to know that I fell at my post of duty, trusting in Him who alone is able to save from sin, who is on our side, aiding in putting down the most black-hearted and damnable rebellion the world ever knew. But I fear I shall weary you with this long, dry letter. I am well and hearty as ever, and can still lift my eyes to the hills whence cometh our salvation. May God prosper our arms and nerve our arms for the great work before us."

While thus promoting the efficiency of his brigade in drill, comfort, and health, in which he succeeded wonderfully, he kept them all alive to the fact that they were soon to fight. General McClellan had given orders to withdraw their outposts to a line nearer Washington; General Kearny expostulated successfully, and kept his troops constantly on the watch. They were the vanguard of the army. His object was to generate military vigilance.

And so the autumn of 1861 rolled on, Kearny and a few like him impatiently longing for the order to advance; Ball's Bluff checking and delaying it, and carrying sorrow and almost dismay to the hearts of the Northern patriots; Drainesville partially reassuring them; the victories south and west invigorating the resolution of the nation; General McClellan bustling hither and thither, reputed busy and successful in organization; the Cabinet, the President, and the nation, waiting long, at first with full, then with scarce half, confidence in the commanding general, for the moment when, with the advance of the Army of the Potomac, the haughty confederacy should disappear.

It was not long, however, before the lynx-like perception of General Kearny saw the truth as to his commanding general, and he expressed it, not insubordinately but confidentially, and with many cautions and generous hopes that he might be mistaken. In October, 1861, he writes: "I see a vacillation in his great objects, allowing small objects to intrude." "That General McClellan," he writes in February, 1862, "has had full sway for his great *specialité*—talents of calculation and long-headedness—is most fortunate for him and the country. But the United States alone of all countries could have supplied by her wonderful virgin resources for a want of genius of command, which would early in September have decided, by timely fighting and maneuvering, what we are doing now by dead momentum. Fifty thousand more troops on the Potomac would have maneuvered the enemy with sure success out of Manassas in September last; England would not have insulted us, foreign powers not been doubtful of us; the greatness of the American name been more immediately vindicated, and the terrific expenses been saved by a speedy termination of the war." March 4th, 1862, he speaks more decidedly.

"Although there is no one exactly to replace McClellan, I now pro. claim distinctly that, unless a chief, a line officer not an engineer, of military prestige, (success under fire with troops,) is put in command of the Army of the Potomac, (leaving McClellan the minor duties of General-in-Chief,) we will come in for some *awful* disaster. The only person to take his place is General C. F. Smith, in the army of Kentucky."

Up to this time he and General McClellan had never clashed. These opinions were the result of his observation, and very much of his conviction that Ball's Bluff was really an advance, from which McClellan shrunk back, and threw the blame on General Stone, unjustly—scared by the first disaster. Not long after he saw himself what he deemed evidence of the inferiority of McClellan's genius, and thenceforward he was most decided in his depreciation of him.

In March, 1862, the rebels evacuated Manassas, hastened thence by the enterprise and dash of General Kearny. It is but justice to notice this, for his reports never saw the light. Indeed that affair, instead of helping his advancement, evidently and most wrongfully retarded it. We will tell the story in his own words, under date of March 12th, 1862. "I was on the Uniform Board, dined with the Prince de Joinville on Thursday; the next day leisurely got up, and went to the ferry to go to camp. I was just going on board the steamer when General Sumner got off, and said quite excitedly and flurried to me, 'Why, your brigade is off, ordered to Burke's Station, to relieve General Howard in guarding a railroad party.' I hurried to camp, found the brigade still there; went to Franklin's headquarters. He was in W——, and by telegraph sent us varying orders from moment to moment, as if all in W—— were undecided. Finally, late in the day orders came to take forty-eight hours' rations, and be prepared to remain two days at Burke's. It was three o'clock. The troops looked elegantly, and, although the march was awful, owing to the roads, they kept up their spirits. It was four o'clock daybreak when I arrived at Burke's. I slept an hour, mounted a fresh horse, and galloped about until twelve with General Howard and others, studying my position. . I then was galloping about, except a nap for two hours, on other fresh horses till nine at night. The next day I ascertained by negroes that the enemy were preparing to leave. I immediately pushed on with my troops, and manœuvered in all directions, all which resulted in my driving them back everywhere. I kept applying for orders, which were not sent me, but still I kept on. General McClellan's whole movement has been thus brought about. I was the first to enter the stronghold at the Junction. My Third New-Jersey planted their flag, and I was returning to Centreville, when I met General McClellan and all his staff, and some 2000 horse, approaching with skirmishers, as if we were secessionists. They had done the same thing in advancing to Fairfax Court-House, which I had taken some twenty-four hours previously."

In approaching Manassas on this occasion General Kearny expanded his brigade over the country, so as to make the enemy think him the van of the whole army. Hence they made a precipitate retreat, leaving the very meal they were about to make untasted, for the use of their adversaries. It was a bold, skillful, and energetic movement, and deserved a commendation which it did not receive. His division commander, he thought, evidently disliked it, and General McClellan suppressed his report, as if not entirely pleased with the occurrence.

But the neglect of McClellan to take advantage of this success by immediately following up the retiring and, to all appearance, surprised enemy, completely satisfied General Kearny of his incompetency. From thenceforward his opinion of him was fixed. "The stupid fact is, (he writes, March 17th, 1862,) that, not content with letting me and others push after the panic-stricken enemy, fighting him a big battle, and ending the war—for his panic promised us sure success—McClellan, so powerful with figures but so weak with men, has brought us all back. It is so like our good old nursery story,

> ' The king of France, with twice ten thousand men,
> Marched up the hill, and then marched down again.'

The result will be that, in Southern character, they will more than recuperate, more than think us afraid of a real stand-up fight, meet us at the prepared points, possibly play ugly tricks at the capital, and nonplus or force us to fight with the worst of chances against us; and all this because when McClellan, out of confidence since *his* failure at Ball's Bluff, despairing of a direct attack on Manassas, invented, with the aid of engineers, (men who are ignorant of soldiers,) the plan of turning the enemy by a sea-route, instead of availing himself of the good luck of the enemy's retreat, thinks that he must still adhere to his sea-plan, like the overstuffed glutton who thinks he must cram because he has in hand an *embarras des richesses.*'"

March 31st, he writes, sketching a campaign for the enemy which was not attempted till Pope's time: "Our present affair is a terrific blunder. Instead of following up, overtaking, and whipping the enemy as they retired panic-stricken, he is attempting an affair of rivers. I do not know his full means of action, but I do know that, if opposed with enterprise, the Southern army, recuperated under the plea of our evading a real fight, will seize Centreville or Manassas, just in rear of the forces left on the Rappahannock, cut them off, restore the uninjured railroad, steam *via* Harper's Ferry to Baltimore and Washington, and be back in time to meet us before Richmond, because the batteries on York and James Rivers, if as formidable as the captured resources of Norfolk should have made them in guns, will oblige us (if we have no ironed armor gunboats) to land our heavy pieces and take them piecemeal, (besides expending thus gratuitously much blood,) all which takes time. I can only account for this absurd movement from General McClellan and his advisers not having sufficient simplicity of character. It would have been so beautiful to have pushed after the enemy, and, in doing so, isolate Fredericksburg, carry it easily, occupy that road, and thus turn those river batteries, all the while near enough to Washington in case of any attempt on it. They will tell you that it was a want of subsistence, etc. This only proves how unpractical McClellan and his advisers are. And it is precisely from a mismanagement of these simple details in our own camps on the Potomac that I have the more and more learned to distrust him entirely. However, Johnston is a very slow man, and our resources are enormous, so we must win, and McClellan will no doubt pass down in history as a great general. What annoys me the most is, that he has stupidly blundered in carrying out his own plans. We should at least have kept the enemy impressed with the idea of our direct advance, and withdrawn division after division in the stealthiness of night and under the curtain of strong corps."

This was an early day for such criticisms. They meant what Grant afterward painfully executed. Some 200,000 men lay round Washington then. The rebel force was barely 40,000. The direct advance would have been necessarily overwhelming. No maneuvers could have resisted it. Looking back, and with the knowledge we now possess, we know that, undertaken then, the direct advance must have been speedily successful, economizing rivers of blood and thousands of lives. Says Pollard in his *Lost Cause*, p. 262: "On March 1st, 1862, the number of Federal troops in and about Washington had increased to 193,142 fit for duty, with a grand aggregate of 221,987. Let us see what was in front of it on the confederate line of defense. General Johnston had in the camps of Centreville and Manassas less than 30,000 men. Stonewall Jackson had been detached with eleven skeleton regiments to amuse the enemy in the Shenandoah Valley. Such was the force that stood in McClellan's path, and deterred him from a blow that at that time might have been fatal to the Southern confederacy."

We have said that McClellan seemed but ill satisfied with the sudden and skillful movement of Kearny upon Manassas. Perhaps it was in consequence of this, but, whatever the reason, in a few days after he tendered him a command, to which, as numbered thirteen on the list of brigadiers, he was long entitled, of a division vacated by the promotion of General Sumner to a corps. General Kearny was more than glad to accept, only desiring that, inasmuch as his First Jersey brigade had been perfected by such toil, expense, and zeal, he should be at liberty to carry it with him, exchanging it for one of Sumner's, which lay close by Franklin, and the consent of whose brigadier was obtained. General McClellan did not discourage the project, but General Franklin at once rejected it; upon which General Kearny, feeling his Jersey Blues to be a trust especially confided to *him*, and realizing their adoration of him, most generously declined the proposition, and, ranking many division generals, remained with his brigade. This conduct was rewarded as might readily be expected. As soon as it was known, in spite of orders to avoid all demonstrations, the enthusiasm of his brave boys could not be restrained. His appearance was the signal for irrepressible cheering. His men would have followed him, or gone at his bidding anywhere against any odds; nor did a Jersey soldier ever forget it

With all this, the step caused General Kearny much regret. His subordination to men of much less military experience than his own perpetually annoyed him. He had strong reliance upon his own powers, a reliance which was by no means conceited, and which was afterward thoroughly justified. Feeling himself equal to almost any task, he could not help longing to take the place of some one of those whom in his confidential correspondence he styled his "inferior superiors." It was some alleviation to his disappointment, and the state of harassed feeling, which his inferior position occasioned, to find himself valued as he was by New-Jersey and its Legislature. How much its patriotic executive regarded him he was not then aware, and his correspondence betrayed an unjust opinion upon that subject. But the press, the people, and the Legislature of New-Jersey, all exhibited their admiration and attachment for him in such a manner as could not be otherwise than gratifying. On the 20th of March, 1862, the Legislature passed a resolution declaring "that New-Jersey highly appreciates the disinterested fidelity of General Philip Kearny in declining proffered promotion rather than separate himself from the command of Jerseymen intrusted to him."

On the 28th of the same month, a set of resolutions was passed, in the following terms: "*Resolved*, That to the New-Jersey volunteers belongs the praise not only of checking the retreat of the Federal forces retiring from Bull Run, and greatly aiding in the preservation of the National Capital from capture, but also of advancing unsupported on the rebel stronghold at Manassas, and compelling its precipitate abandonment; and that General Kearny deserves the warm approval and thanks of the nation for his boldness in making this advance, and the skillful strategy he displayed in its execution.

"*Resolved*, That, having already testified our high appreciation of the self-sacrifice and fidelity to his trust which led General Kearny to decline promotion rather than leave his brigade, we now express our regret at the existence of any such necessity, and respectfully suggest to those in authority the propriety (unless it be inconsistent with the public interest) of combining all the New-Jersey troops on the Potomac into one division, and placing the same under the command of General Kearny, whose devotion to his soldiers, care for their comfort and discipline, and brilliant qualities as an officer, entitle the country to his services in a higher position than the one he occupies.

"*Resolved*, That a copy of these resolutions be forwarded to the Honorable the Secretary of War."

The idea contained in the second of these resolutions was a favorite one with General Kearny, who believed our troops would fight better if brigaded by States; but the fear that State pride might occasion dissension made the plan unpalatable at Washington.

The delays he expected when he discovered the route McClellan had determined upon were even more tedious than he anticipated. It was not until the 26th of April that he found himself near Yorktown, on board of a splendid steamer, waiting to land, and fretting himself over the want of practical skill which, as he said, sickened his soldiers by cooping them on the transport, because they dared not hazard a landing under fire. While on board, a vacancy happened in a division of Heintzelman's corps. Our army lay before Yorktown; the division was actually under fire; so General Kearny regarded himself as bound to assume at once the position to which he was ordered, and with grief which he could not conceal, in the midst of actual tears from the brigade so long his pride and so long his worshipers, he laid down his command of the Jersey troops, and thenceforward was known no longer as their general. This was on the 30th day of April. He assumed command on the 2d day of May. On the 5th, he fought the great battle of Williamsburg, inflicting upon the enemy their first decided defeat by the army of the Potomac, and saving that army from hopeless ruin.

Yorktown was evacuated on the night of the 3d of May. Eleven thousand men under General Magruder, who adopted here the stratagem of Kearny when approaching Manassas, and extended his little force over a distance of several miles, so as to give it the appearance of large numbers, had delayed nearly 90,000 infantry, 50 batteries of artillery, 10,000 cavalry, and a siege-train of 100 guns, from the 4th day of April previous. The fact is proof enough of the correctness of Kearny's opinion, both as to the folly of the route and the incompetency of his commander.

As soon as the evacuation was discovered, General McClellan pursued the enemy up the peninsula, over such terrible roads, and with such a want of disciplined organization, that the army was more a mass of straggling men than a systematic array. Says Pollard: "The pursuing army toiled on through rain falling in torrents, over roads deep in mud, the men straggling, falling out, and halting without orders, the artillery, cavalry, infantry, and baggage intermingled in apparently inexplicable confusion." Hooker, also of Heintzelman's corps, was in the advance, Kearny far in the rear; between them was Sumner's corps of some 30,000 men, besides other troops. Magruder stood at bay at the fort which bears his name; a severe action began, and Hooker was hardly pressed. He sent to Sumner for reënforcements. Sumner, under orders which the commanding general had given him, dared not, or at least did not, send him any troops. The message was forwarded to Kearny, and we shall let him describe his services in his own words : "At a quarter to eleven A.M., an order was received from General Sumner to pass all the others, and proceed to the support of General Hooker, already engaged. With difficulty and loss of time, my division at length made its way through the mass of troops and trains that encumbered the deep, muddy defile, until at Brick Church my route was to the left. At half-past one, within three and a half miles of the battle-field, I halted my column to rest for the first time, and to get the lengthened files in command before committing them to action. Almost immediately, however, on orders from General Heintzelman, our knapsacks were piled, and the head of the column resumed its march, taking the double-quick wherever the mud-holes would allow a footing. Arrived at one mile from the engagement, I received an order for detaching three regiments to the left position. Approaching nearer, word was brought by an aid that Hooker's cartridges were expended, and with increased rapidity we entered under fire. Having quickly consulted with General Hooker, I deployed one brigade on the left of the Williamsburg road, another on its right, taking, to cover them and support the remaining battery that had ceased to fire, two companies of another regiment. As our troops came into action, they passed the remnants of the brave men of Hooker, and commenced an unremitting, well-directed fire. However, from the lengthening of the files, a gap was occasioned by the withdrawal of three regiments from the column and the silence of this battery, and I was soon left no alternative but to lead forward to the charge two companies of Michigan volunteers to drive back the enemy's sharp-shooters, now crowding upon our pieces. This duty was performed, and enabled Major Wainwright, of Hooker's division, to collect his artillerists and reopen fire from several pieces. A new support was then collected from the Fifth Jersey, who, terribly decimated previously, again came forward with alacrity. Our forces were now successfully engaged, and kept steadily gaining ground; but the heaviness of the timber of the *abatis* defied all direct approach, and, after advancing fresh marksmen from Poe's regiment, I ordered the Thirty-eighth New-York to charge down the road and take the pieces in the centre of the *abatis* by their flank. This duty was performed; still, the wave of impulsion, though nearly successful, did not quite prevail, but every point gained was fully sustained. The left wing of the Fortieth New-York was next sent for. It came up, conducted by Captain Mindil * of Birney's staff, charged up to the appointed space, silenced some light artillery, and, gaining the enemy's rear, caused him to relinquish his works. The victory was ours. About this period, General Jameson brought up the rear brigade and detached regiments, and a second line was established, and two columns of regiments made disposable for further moves; but darkness, with the still drizzling rain, now closed in, and the regiments bivouacked on the field they had won. The reconnoissance during the night and the early patrols of the morning revealed the enemy retreating; the enemy's works were entered, and the position taken in full force."

General Kearny's forces in this battle were entirely disproportionate to his success. He entered with five regiments, from all of whom many men had straggled, leaving him at the first the sum of 1900 men. In his correspondence he says: "We dashed in at double-quick, our band playing, and, rather reckless of myself, I located my men right, leading them off personally from the word *go*. At the outset, seeing that time was pressing, I charged back the mass of the enemy's sharp-shooters, who thought the field their own, our pieces having been abandoned by the gunners, with only two companies, barely eighty men. But I remembered that such things had been done before, and had no alternative, for my regiments had never from morning been allowed to close up; and so off I went, too conspicuous from my showy horse, and for several hundred yards down the road, with bristling *abatis* on each side, filled with the enemy's marksmen. This, like all such things, only succeeded because the enemy presumes them, few as they are, the precursors of crowds behind."

It was the source of the deepest mortification to General Kearny that his services on this occasion seemed entirely unappreciated by his commanding officer. When the battle took place, General McClellan was far in the rear. The importunity of Governor Sprague prevailed on him to go to the front, and he arrived in time to witness the gallantry of Hancock, engaged far on the right, and who, charging

---

* Since Brigadier-General Mindil, Colonel of New-Jersey Thirty-third.

with his whole brigade just at dusk, contributed, with the loss of only thirty men, to the final victory. The entire Federal loss was 2228. Two thirds of this fell upon Hooker, the rest upon Kearny, demonstrating where the real fighting had been; yet, in his first bulletin, General McClellan, though informed by his own aid of the facts, (so Kearny says,) absolutely failed even to mention either Hooker or Kearny, to their great and just indignation, for the success at Williamsburg evidently saved the army. Huddled in confused masses, the artillery fastened in the mud, the infantry straggling and wading through the woods, the cavalry, baggage-wagons, and all the paraphernalia of an advance confusedly edging along through miry roads, panic would have been ruin. Scarce any of the troops had ever been in action, and, had the enemy been victorious, a panic would have been almost unavoidable, and General Kearny felt that he had prevented this by the utmost hazard of his person. He was not proud of recklessness, but he knew that there were times when exposure was essential. "It is true," he writes, "that I was fearfully exposed; for, whilst the entire regiment would be sheltered by logs, I was the only officer mounted and quite in view, the only object aimed at by many hardly fifty feet from me. I could not do otherwise, for we had the largest part of the work before us, and very few to do it. It was not useless recklessness; it saved the day."

General Kearny expected a rapid advance from Williamsburg; he knew the discomfiture and panic of the rebels. Instant pursuit and the following of it up would, in his opinion, have enabled us either to enter Richmond with them, or, at least, gain the advantage of position; but again he found nothing but tardiness and delay. The distance from Williamsburg was a little more than forty miles. On the eighth, three days after the battle, our troops collected there began to move, and in two days they marched nineteen miles. On the thirteenth, the army was concentrated near West-Point, and not until the twentieth did Stoneman's cavalry reach the Chickahominy at New-Bridge, whilst the main forces were not in position until the twenty-fourth. The camp of General Kearny was established on the Williamsburg road, near Bottom's Bridge, over the Chickahominy. Casey's division of Keyes's corps crossed the twentieth of April, and Heintzelman's corps, including Kearny's division, was thrown forward in support, and Bottom's Bridge rebuilt, to connect them with the main army. These forces were a part of our left wing; the right wing had been thrown well forward, in order, so McClellan states, to insure a junction with McDowell's force, which he expected from Fredericksburg. The operation, as will be seen by the map, placed the Chickahominy between the wings of the army; the Second Corps were on the right bank of that stream, the Third on the left, and, thus situated, the quick eye of Kearny saw and prophesied the dangers. On the twenty-eighth day of May he writes to a correspondent as follows: "And now for our present affairs. They seem to move on tolerably, but without vitality, and with hourly signs of a want of talent and administration. We are likely to have a full battle in a very few hours. I confess myself not over-sanguine about it. By mismanagement the army has lost one third (by sickness and stragglers) since leaving Yorktown. Those brigades within my hearing only average about two thousand, instead of over three thousand; they should be four thousand. But this is not all. McClellan, most unfortunately, is putting up, every three or four miles or less, successive lines of rifle-pits, miles in length, thus too openly imparting to the soldiers his own personal distrust of them." In another letter he writes thus: "We are on the eve of a great battle, which is to decide the fate of Virginia. The enemy will fight well, although shaken by the defeat at Williamsburg. I presume that, after our lead-off the other day, the rest of the army will fight well; but McClellan has been most injudicious with his ill-organized marches, and easy permission to the men to escape home and be sent back on the slightest pretext of sickness. McClellan has been too slow; he should have annihilated the enemy in Williamsburg before they could have reached the Chickahominy. Until within three days he evidently had no fixed plan of action; since then he has done better. The battle will be on Wednesday. Unless a Bull Run, it will be a full success; if a Bull Run, I expect that my division will be the only one to escape. I have my men completely in hand; they became very enthusiastic for me, but I have seen so much mismanagement that nothing will take me unawares." We did have "a full battle in a very few hours"; it was the battle of Fair Oaks, called by the rebels Seven Pines. Fair Oaks is a station on the railroad; Seven Pines a locality close by, where Keyes, commanding our advance corps, was intrenched. Johnston, then in command of the rebel forces, learning only on the thirtieth of May that Keyes's corps was upon the Richmond side of the stream, resolved to attack it the next morning, hoping to be able to defeat Keyes's corps completely in his advanced position before it could be reënforced. The attack was to be made by four full divisions—Huger, Longstreet, D. H. Hill, and G. W. Smith—comprising forty-eight thousand men. The main assault was to be made in front by Longstreet, with his own division and that of Hill; Huger was to move down the Charles City road, and attack the left flank of the force engaged by Longstreet, while Smith was to march to the junction of New-Bridge and Nine Mile roads, and be ready to assail the right flank of Keyes and cover Longstreet's left. On the night of the twenty-ninth, a violent storm occurred; the Chickahominy was swollen and overflowed; the left wing of the Union army, greatly over-matched by the numbers of the enemy, seemed doomed to destruction. The attack was to be made at daybreak, but Huger, prevented by the swollen stream, did not come up. At a late hour of the day, Longstreet determined to move with his own and with Hill's division, and accomplish whatever results were possible. Casey's division was in advance at Fair Oaks farm, three quarters of a mile in front of Seven Pines, its pickets being pushed one third of a mile further up to the edge of the wood which screened the enemy from view. There being indications of an impending attack, Keyes ordered his division to be under arms at eleven o'clock. Receiving news that the enemy were coming down the Williamsburg road, Casey advanced several batteries to meet them, and sent back for reënforcements. He had scarcely done this when the enemy burst through the woods. His pickets and following regiments were swept back in confusion. To save his guns, a charge was made upon the enemy, which was met with a furious fire of musketry, and forced back. The guns were saved, excepting one, and then the whole division fell back to the line of defense at Fair Oaks farm, one third of a mile behind. Here they stood for three hours, but at length fell back three quarters of a mile further to Seven Pines, then held by Couch's division. This retreat was made just in time; as it was, they lost a battery of five guns. Couch's division, at Seven Pines, had been weakened by send-ing regiments to support Casey; their line of defense lay across the road; their corps commander, Keyes, brought forward reënforce-ments and made a stand; but Longstreet's force, coming up, assailed the line in front and on both flanks, and Couch was forced from his position, and withdrew to Fair Oaks station, where he took part in the action just begun at that point. Kearny's division now came upon the field, and sustained the almost discomfited Union forces until about five o'clock, when they again gave way and fell back from Seven Pines. How Kearny came up, and what part he took in the battle, we will now let him tell in his own words: "As the battle came off quite unexpectedly yesterday, I hasten to send you a line, knowing how anxious you will be, and to say that I thank God that the great risks (for it was again a crisis of saving a runaway people) I ran have not resulted in even a light wound. I was visiting some friends the other side of the Chickahominy, some five or six miles off, when a rattle of musketry was heard, and I instantly felt that I was concerned in it. So, mounting, I galloped back, and was just in time to lead my men some miles to the front, to save a huge corps that had run like good fellows at the first attack. This time it was an old acquaintance in Mexico, General Casey, whose men gave way most shamefully—filling the roads from the battle-field to our camp, three and a half miles—and ran away worse than at Bull Run. I am used to many strange sights, but, when I saw before the race of the fugitives a whole line of wagons going full tilt, I thought that many a pretty bold man might well have his senses turned. Then came a stream of fugitives, and finally they poured in in masses. My superior, Heintzelman, had previously ordered me to leave a brigade in the rear. He then first sent to me to send away one brigade by the railroad, quite away from my control, and then a brigade up to the battle-field. I accompanied this, ordered, at my own responsibility, my absent brigade, (Jameson's,) and pushed on at a fearful pace. I got under fire, as usual, and was sent to *charge*, whilst thousands of those I came to help were left quietly to be passed by, by me, and crouch down in the rifle-pits and fortifications. We put right in, and I drove back the enemy; but McClellan's injustice has changed my men. They followed me, after a fashion, but were cold and slow ; still, I won every thing. When the enemy got behind us, and the troops in the rear ran like sheep, I flew to them, hurrahed at them, waved my cap, and, turning them, led them into the fight again. I had hardly done this, when another large party of the enemy stole in behind my brigade, and I was nearly cut off from my own men; but, rushing to a wood near by, I made a stand. However, I looked back at my recent borrowed followers, and found them and all the others—some seven or eight thousand— of that line (Keyes's corps) running like good fellows, and masses of the enemy regularly, but surely, rapidly, and sternly, pursuing them, keeping the only reported roads of retreat. Thinks I to myself, I am cut off, *me and mine.* Most fortunately, I had that very morning examined, with a fine guide, all that secret, locked-up country of forests and swamps. I saw that they hoped to cut me off from re- treat by getting between me and White Oak swamp. By this time a regiment of mine, attracted by the firing in their rear, came along in the woods. I charged the enemy in rear, and would have gained the day but for continuous reënforcements. But I fought them long enough to enable all my intercepted regiments to retire by a secret road through the swamp; got back to my position—a very strong one, from which I should not have been taken—before the enemy arrived there, and again offered the sole barrier when all else was confusion. Still, this was not victory. It was the first time that I had not slept on the battle-field, and, but for the mismanagement as to our battle at Williamsburg, I would have been victorious here too ; still, it is most infecting to be sent for to restore a fight, and see hordes of others panic-stricken, disobedient, craven, and down- cast. Anywhere, it is a disagreeable sight to see the wounded being carried off the field of battle—even from a victorious one. I have again had an aid wounded, and lost my beautiful bay colt, which was shot from under me. I was not so long, but at times more exposed than ever; my colt, being very fractious, kept me, while plunging, in a perfect current of cannon and rifle balls, and alone in the face of too many scamps, who seemed to pick me out. It was at this time that my colt received his first wound; an hour later he was killed under me, and I mounted the horse of an adjutant who chanced to follow."

While this battle was going on, Sumner, receiving orders from General McClellan six miles away, advanced two divisions across the rapidly swelling river, and with another (Sedgwick's) pushed on to Fair Oaks station; there met General Couch, and formed a line along the north side of the railroad, from the station eastward. At five o'clock, the enemy opened a furious attack upon his centre, hoping to get possession of a battery of artillery there posted. The early twilight was just closing in, when Sumner charged with six regiments, directly into the woods, and hurled the enemy back in confusion. At this moment, General Johnston, who was overseeing the battle there, was severely wounded, and carried from the field. The next day the attack was fiercely renewed, repulsed, and again renewed, but without success. Meanwhile Hooker, coming up from the left, found Kearny's forces, a brigade of General Birney, drawn up in line of battle, and with these fell upon the enemy's rear, after an hour's hard fighting pushed them through the woods, then ordered a bayonet charge, and the enemy broke and fled toward Richmond. Sumner's force, at the same time, further advanced, and charged, giving them victory there. The Confederates retired upon the forces who had the day before gained the battle of Seven Pines, and the whole army moved back, utterly foiled in the object for which the attack had been made, broken and dispirited. It is now well known that, had McClellan been aware how utterly broken it was, he might have marched straight on to Richmond on the 1st of June. Its approaches were totally unfortified. Hooker and Kearny were both earnest, not only in opinion, but in requesting McClellan to pursue the enemy and to take Richmond. Hooker advanced the day after, a mile or more toward Richmond, meeting no resistance, but was recalled by a telegram that he should return from his brilliant reconnoissance, "We can not afford to lose his division," and then a long delay again. Fair Oaks, first a disaster, and then, by dint of the exertions of Kearny on the first day, and of Hooker and Kearny on the second, turned into victory, gave our arms no real advantage. Our army went to rest in the swamps of the Chickahominy, dying with disease, rusting with inaction; the country still looking on patiently and full of faith, hopeful each day of some crowning victory. We again recur to the correspondence of General Kearny. Under date of the 22d of June, he writes as follows: "I am sorry that I can not give you interesting news. Here we are again at a dead-lock; Manassas over again; both parties intrenched up to their eyes; both waiting for something; unluckily, our adversaries gaining two to our one. Our last chance to conquer Richmond —for Dame Fortune is resentful of slighted charms—was thrown away when our great battle of Fair Oaks was thrown away. We had tempted the enemy to attack us whilst divided by the Chickahominy. Fortunately, he failed. The prestige, nearly lost to us by our inaction since Williamsburg, was once more in the ascendency. It only required McClellan to put forth moral force and his military might, and Richmond would have been ours. But no; delay on delay, fortifications, as if we were beaten, met by stronger counter-fortifications, on points previously neglected; undue concentration of our troops on points already over-manned, met by a net-work enveloping us by them; supineness in our camps, met by daring forays by them; the boasted influence of our reserve artillery, counterbalanced by their availing themselves of the respite to get up artillery even of greater calibre; the reliance on further troops from the North more than met by reënforcements of two to one by their recalling troops from the South. Indeed, every thing so betokens fear on the part of the general commanding, and the enemy show themselves so emboldened, that, with the numbers crowding up around us, I am puzzled to divine the next act of the drama. *It will be either another inexplicable evacuation, or the suffocation of this army by the seizure of our communications when least expected.* The enemy wish us to attack. McClellan has proved by his fortifications that he is feeble. We are surrounded in front by a cordon of troops and forts. It is true that they will fail if they attack us; but, if they do not do that, they will leave enough troops in our front, and, crossing the Chickahominy, *cut us off from our lines of communication and sustenance.*" As before Fair Oaks, we have seen General Kearny prophesying a battle, and expressing his apprehension that, owing to the careless manner in which the troops were arranged, some would be cut off, almost the picture of what really did occur; so here we have him, not a week before, prophesying the foray of Jackson, and anticipating that magnificent attack upon our communications which resulted in the far-famed "change of base," and brought with it almost ruin to the hopes of the Union.

It would be impossible and even useless here to recite the history of those dreadful seven days of retreat, disaster, and confusion; daily victory and nightly retreat, strewing the roads through which our army dragged its weary way with the dead and wounded and dying; those never-to-be-forgotten fights, Gaines's Mills, Savage's Station, Glendale, and, last of all, Malvern Hill, at the three last of which victory was really with us, but in each of which we, by retreating, basely acknowledged defeat; from the last two of which, certainly the last, the army might, with a leader of any nerve, have marched straight to the coveted prize—Richmond. It would be useless, I say, to recite the horrors and glories of those unparalleled fields, and particularize the efforts and successes which attended the fighting division of "Fighting Phil Kearny." Suffice it to say that his troops were always engaged; his commanding eye always busy; his successes always resplendent, even when all around was defeat; and that he always purchased what he earned by the same high qualities of indomitable courage, sustained by self-exposure, inspiring his men at once by the skill which they saw him display, and by the fearlessness and magnanimity with which he always went wherever he declared it their duty to go. These battles were not planned or fought by the commanding general. At no one time, except for a short time at Malvern Hill, was he ever present; his participation consisted in determining the points where stands would be made by the regiments; the battle would be made by the commanders under him; and each for the most part took care of his own division or his corps. Sad days were those, not only for the army, whose bravery was never more resplendent, but for the people, whose eyes beheld the worthlessness of all upon which they relied, who mourned a son or friend in every hamlet and in almost every house, and at the end stood appalled and paralyzed, not knowing whence relief could come, and who might have given up the contest, but for their unfaltering trust that a cause so right could not perish.

It will be more interesting, and more in accordance with our present purpose, to resume again the correspondence of General Kearny, and thence derive our acquaintance with his military character. A letter of anxious inquiry had been written to him respecting the fate of Major Ryerson,* of Sussex, reported at first to have fallen. Under date of the 10th of July, from Harrison's Landing, he writes as follows: "Your request as to Major Ryerson's effects shall be attended to; but I am glad to have it from reliable sources that he is a prisoner, and not dangerously though badly wounded. The siege of Richmond was raised, and here we are drifting down the stream. How curious all this verification of prognostications I so correctly read, and yet feared to translate; so strangely correct have been my instincts in this war as in previous ones. In Italy, in 1859, it was the same thing, and made my betters sometimes wonder; but this war is plain to those who, with experience, will take pains to

---

* Afterward killed at the "Wilderness."

look danger in the face, to leave little to mere hope, and remember that a Southern army can not afford to be idle. Our coming here has been a most cowardly and unwise alternative. The battles on the left bank of the Chickahominy were mismanaged. I had been over there several days before, and observed to all around how we would be strategically and tactically whipped; attacked from an inland point not provided against, and be thrown down-hill, and then have to work up again, and be thus crippled and destroyed. It occurred so precisely. Then comes the fearful error of McClellan's want of nerve. Instead of *instanter* reducing his line of defense to a certain intrenched *tête-de-pont* on the right bank, merely covering Bottom's Bridge and the railroad bridge, and beyond which he never should have made a *serious* advance short of adopting an attack and rushing into Richmond by that side—a *tête-de-pont* fully fortified and strong; and crossing the night of the first, or certainly the second battle, when he could no longer have been deceived, *all his troops*, except the 10,000 men requisite for the *tête-de-pont*, to the left bank, there to defy and give a general battle—and the ground was admirable for us; then, in case of victory, recrossing and rushing into Richmond; in case of defeat, retiring, as other beaten armies do, back along his line of communications, to his basis of operations, be it to White House, be it to Williamsburg, be it to Yorktown; thus always firm, always secure, always covering his own supply, always embarrassing his enemy by drawing them on when they have no transportation to follow, when they dare not leave Richmond too far. Instead of all this, as simple as the pursuit of the panic-stricken army running from Manassas, he loses head and heart, throws himself back on the shipping, and gulls the silly public with a hard name, namely, that he has changed his base of operations. This is false, and by this time he knows it. We have no basis whatever to act on. As to ascending the James, when, after the successful fight at Malvern Hill, he yielded the strongest battle-field that we have yet had, he gave to the enemy a fearfully strong position which debars our future advance. As to crossing the James river, that is out of the question. It would result in nothing, but only the more endanger Washington. And now I distinctly assure you that there are ninety-nine chances in a hundred of Washington's being taken in less than fifteen days. But the falsity of the James river being a base of operations is this, that it is quietly known that, if there were full peace, the James river has been so effectively obstructed that it could not be cleared under many weeks; besides, gunboats are overrated. The enemy fought very cowardly in the West, hence their success. In this region the rebels face full batteries on the open ground, hurling grape at them, and come up to the muzzles of the guns. This was the case on the 30th ult., on the New-Market road, where nothing but my so-called personal rashness in heading the Sixty-third Pennsylvania and a part of the Thirty-seventh New-York, in leading them to the charge, saved my pieces. To me the most cruel thing of this war is the unhandsome attempt of crushing my military mastery of my profession under the decrying epithets of rashness. My best results of head would often fail but for the stimulus of my lead. No; very far from having a base to act on, General McClellan has *boxed* us. You will soon hear of the James river being rendered impassable for our supplies, and then, like drowned rats, we must soon come out of our holes. But it will be done with more awful sacrifices, of useless because avoidable battles. We are fortifying here again, unnecessarily so. It breaks the hearts of the soldiers, gives them the idea that they can not win fields, and yet in a few days, sooner or later, we will have to burst through the network that the enemy are preparing around us, and, if we do not, look out for Washington. That city will go. They will crush Pope, by leaving McClellan in ignorance of their departure, then for a foreign alliance, and good-night to the North. Even now McClellan's defeat will be likely to produce this. His 'change of base' may cheat the American neswpapers and fool the American people; but the ignominious retreat, the abandonment of the sick and wounded, the abandonment of stores, and loss of strategical supremacy can not be concealed from military eyes in France, England, nor elsewhere. So much for McClellan and the politicians.

"P.S.—One curious fact: knowing the ease of carrying off my sick and wounded from Fair Oaks, (I sent them off early,) I was ordered to unload them and abandon them ; but I did not, and carried them off, but, although I had twenty empty wagons, was prevented taking off those of another hospital. Fortunately, they, too, principally got clear."

I will not apologize for extracting this long letter. There is much in it to exhibit the peculiarities of General Kearny's character. Next to his sense of the disgrace inflicted upon the army at large, and the country, by the retreat which he so severely denounced, was his grief at the losses and almost ruin of his pet Jersey brigade, upon whose fate he ever looked with parental anxiety. "I am sickened," he writes in a letter of July 24th, "by the falseness of the times, and the gratuitous sacrifice of the Jersey brigade is enough to make me so. Why did not their division general go to command in person? It was his own part of the division, (Slocum's.) It was half of his provisional corps, and surely why not place it in the fight, even if he did no more? There is some awful secret history to this Slocum's division at Friday's fight. You will learn it in the end; the battle which had been won was lost by imbecility." July 31st, he writes: "Major Ryerson is home to tell his own story, and more have escaped than we counted on. I am much affected by two circumstances, the loss of the colors of the Second regiment, and the surrender of the Fourth, with scarcely a man hurt, all of which only proves the want of confidence incident on a want of military management on the part of the noblest troops on the earth, my old brigade, in that disastrous battle of the 27th of June, on the Chickahominy. General Taylor tells a sad story of it; the brave Hexamer, of the battery, even worse; and yet McClellan screens Porter, and Congress brevets him. As to their commanding general, I can not understand how a general like him, with his legitimate division, one half of his command committed to fight under his own eye, in his very presence, and that he should have never taken charge of their welfare. At Williamsburg, I engaged the enemy with but five regiments, and at Fair Oaks with but one brigade, and yet this is set down as rashness of my own person. I dislike to think of this, the noblest brigade in the army, frittered to shreds in a moment. How truly and honestly would I have served under General Cook, had Jersey but united her soldiers for us.

"Our great anniversary is hardly past, recalling most painfully the uprising of the North at this epoch last year, till then much treachery, but not a reverse of arms. How vividly do I recall, in an oration I heard that day, the truthful tribute to General Scott, as the only man who could have impressed with certain victory the mass of his countrymen, who, had he been left in general control, would have mesmerized us with his own unrivaled conviction of success. But where are we now? Whither has gone the dignity of the finest army ever raised in the hemisphere, if I may not say the world? All disappeared, as if wilted by the touch of some evil genius's wand. An army victorious in retreat, even brilliantly so in the advance, and even in the false position into which it had been exposed, more lavish of blood than aught history presents on record; and yet all this timorously placed in a *cul-de-sac* of which the enemy holds the strings.

"I am glad," he proceeds, "to hear you boldly mention the principle of drafts. Believe me, without it, not only is the Union imperiled, but I will not answer for the existence of the North. The Southerners have long years proclaimed that they could of all people the best sustain a war. Is the North to shut her eyes to the past, and forget Sparta and the Helots, a fighting aristocracy, and the cultivator a slave? The slothfulness of the North, the schisms of its politicians, the trifling of all—in fine, this crisis, dictated by small men of small motives, has developed in the South confidence, and increased venom and the activity of hopefulness, even more than the spasmodic action of despair. They have boldly launched into the experiment which Washington dared not, even for our sacred Revolution; and they have invented the conscription, in which they have succeeded by terrorism, or as likely because, from our temporizing, the South is united to a man; and thus from being weak, comparatively, in population, it is they who outnumber us at present, and will do so the more each succeeding day. Do not be deceived by big words; we have been blinded by them too long. Do not believe that you can starve them by intercepting railroads. In the first place, the position of any railroad argues an unlimited concentration against the assailant, a speedy return to another quarter. But that apart, do not let us fancy that if, for thirty years, all Germany was overrun by armies, living as they went; if that same country was more recently the theatre of war for twenty years of the vast forces of Napoleonic times, and with armies that moved with hardly a provision train, there is any starving an army in the heart of Virginia, where, cut what roads you may, you still have manifold branches near at hand. Besides, look out! the war will be carried into Egypt, and our own purse-strings will be unfastened with a vengeance.

"Why we hesitate, I cannot imagine. It is fearful infatuation to wait. The people are ripe for it, as you remark. Of course they are. First, they are earnest as patriots; and next, they have an instinct of the storm brewing in the horizon. Why the enemy leave us as long alone really embarrasses me; not but that it is very certain that their tremendous, unparalleled daring in facing our artillery has been attended with unparalleled loss. Though successful on the Chickahominy against Porter; unsuccessful, on the 30th of June, on the New-Market road; by the spirited advance of the Sixty-third Pennsylvania and half the Thirty-seventh New-York, which I led up against ten times our number, who, unchecked by the ceaseless discharge of six pieces firing grape, nearly reached the muzzles as soon as ourselves; again unsuccessful at Malvern Heights, from its amphitheatre shape, permitting a concentration of our overnumerous artillery, (the only battle where it has come well into play,) the result of all which was, for the moment, that they could no longer force their men to an immediate repetition. I myself think that they can never repeat it, for it is unusual in war; it is against the axioms of Napoleon as to the capabilities of human courage. Still, their losses, though surpassing ours, are more than made good."

The same letter contains General Kearny's views on a question then much mooted—the employment of negroes in aid of the Union cause. He says : "But besides drafting, it is time for us to deprive the enemy of their extraneous engines of war. There is no more Southern man at heart than myself. I am so from education, association, and from being a purely unprejudiced lover of the Union. But this is now no longer time for hesitation. As the blacks are the rural military force of the South, so should they indiscriminately be received, if not seized and sent off. I would not arm them, but I would use them to spare our whites, needed with their colors ; needed to drill, that first source of discipline—that first utility in battle. But in furtherance of this, instead of the usual twenty pioneers per regiment, I would select fifty stalwart blacks ; give them the ax, the pick, and the spade. But give them high military organization. We want bands—give twenty blacks—again military organization. So, too, cooks for the companies, teamsters—even artillery drivers. Do not stop there—and always *without arms*—organize engineer regiments of blacks for the fortifications, pontoon regiments of blacks, black hospital corps of nurses. Put this in practice, and the day that, from European interference, we have to look *bitterness* nearly in the face, *then*, and not till then, awaken to the conviction that you have an army of over fifty thousand *highly* disciplined soldiery—superior to double the number of our ordinary run of badly diciplined, badly officered, unreliable regiments now intrusted with the fortunes of the North. I would seek French officers for them, from their peculiar gift over "natives." In their own service they easily beat the Arabs—and then officer them and surpass their own troops in desperate valor. Also, I should advise some Jamaica sergeants of the black regiments. As for the women, employ them in hospitals, and in making cartridges, etc. I know the Southern character intimately. It is not truly brave. It is at times desperate, invincible if successful—most dispirited if the reverse—is intimidated at a distant idea, which they would encounter, if suddenly brought to them, face to face. This idea of black adjuncts to the military awakens nothing inhuman. It but prevents the slave, run away or abandoned to us, from becoming a moneyed pressure upon us. It eventually would prepare them for freedom ; for surely we do not intend to give them to their rebel masters. In fine, why have we even now many old soldiers on the frontier garrisons ? Send there a black regiment on trial—not at once, but gradually—by the process I named above. Do this, and besides acquiring a strong provisional army, you magnify your present one by over fifty thousand men."

The spirit of General Kearny was much injured by the disastrous "seven days" from Fair Oaks to Harrison's Landing. He saw victory thrown away, thousands of gallant lives expended, millions of treasure wasted, all from incompetency, and, as he thought himself compelled to believe, a semi-treasonable political creed, while still no change was made, and in truth he himself could see no man on whom the country should dare to rely. And he thought his own services unappreciated, and deserved promotion hopeless. He himself had ever been victor. It is a fact that his division never failed to carry their object. He knew that whatever glory belonged to his corps was earned mainly by himself and Hooker. He saw many unsuccessful men advanced, while he was utterly ignored. Over and over again does he speak in his letters with haughty disgust of the "small men of small motives" who managed this great war. And he began seriously to think that he should "no longer consent to be their puppet." His life at Harrison's Bar was one of comparative rest. In his letters home he describes with enthusiasm the beauties of the scenery, and encourages the loved ones from whom he was absent by descriptions of the comparative comfort he enjoyed. But he was anxious to be rid of the leadership of McClellan. And the time soon came.

The ominous absence of attack from the enemy soon revealed itself. The rebel general, leaving our forces, as Kearny satirically expresses it, "boxed up like herrings," gathered all his own for an attack on Pope. Before the authorities at Washington fully divined his object, McClellan was ordered to withdraw from the peninsula. On his demurring, the order became peremptory, and was obeyed. Heintzelman, with Kearny and Hooker, was the advance-guard of the movement. On the 19th of August, Kearny reached Yorktown, "after some forced marching," he says, "in the wrong direction, ennuied and sick." On the 25th, he joined General Pope, and entered upon his final campaign, its hero, and alas! its victim.

His health at this time was by no means good. He complained in his correspondence that, except when in the saddle, he was almost incapable of exertion; that he returned from wearisome riding so exhausted as to be compelled to throw himself down and rest, without power of self-renewal; and he several times expresses his wonder that when on horseback (where, without exaggeration, were his headquarters) all his ailments seemed to pass away, and he found himself possessed of his accustomed energy. With ill health, there was much depression of spirits. Disappointed by the failure of our arms, utterly faithless in his commanding general, disgusted with an apparent want of appreciation of himself, and with the prodigious waste of our wonderful resources, he entered upon this campaign with alertness, because it was under a new commander, but yet not with that assurance of success which usually made his military life his greatest happiness.

To understand the connection of General Kearny with Pope's campaign, it will be necessary briefly to review some well-known events which occurred previously to Kearny's reaching him.

A short time before General McClellan effected his "change of base," the War Department had gathered together the disjointed forces in Northern Virginia, under Banks, McDowell, and Fremont, and consolidated them into the "Army of Virginia," under General John Pope. On assuming command, he concentrated his forces and threw them, some fifty thousand strong, in front of Washington, along the line of the Orange and Alexandria Railroad in the direction of Gordonsville and Charlottesville. To prevent the seizure of those important points, necessary to his communication with Southwestern Virginia, Lee sent forward the untiring Jackson with General Ewell, and afterward A. P. Hill. On the 7th and 8th of August, Jackson crossed the Rapidan and moved toward Culpeper. Pope advanced Banks to meet him, toward Cedar Mountain, and there occurred the battle so-named, where Banks manfully struggled with superior forces, and, though defeated, stood firm until Jackson withdrew to Gordonsville. This was on the 11th of August. The previous orders to McClellan to leave the Peninsula were urgently repeated while these operations were going on, and their necessity became more evident daily. Lee soon learned of the evacuation, and hastened with all the rapidity he could command, to reach at once the army of General Pope, and defeat it before it could be reënforced. Expecting this, Pope retired nearer Washington, to meet the reënforcements proposed to him, and the better, at the same time, to check the enemy, withdrew behind the Rappahannock. General Lee, finding its fords covered, left Longstreet there to mask a turning movement by Jackson on Pope's right by the way of Warrenton. Jackson accordingly ascended the river and crossed the head of his column (Early's Brigade) at Sulphur or Warrenton Springs on the 22d of August, while Stuart was thrown forward with 1500 cavalry, and swiftly passed around to the rear of our army at Catlett's Station, firing the camp, and actually capturing Pope's official papers and baggage. Jackson's flank march up the Rappahannock was met by a corresponding movement of Pope up the opposite bank, so that on the 24th August, Sigel, Banks, and Reno occupied Sulphur Springs, while Jackson lay on the opposite side of the stream; but on the 25th, Jackson struck out further to his left, crossed the upper Rappahannock, turned Pope's right, and bivouacked at Salem. Marching thirty-five miles next day, diverging eastward, he crossed the Bull Run Mountain through Thoroughfare Gap, a narrow defile near Gainesville, and at sunset he reached Bristoe Station, on the Orange and Alexandria Railroad, a point considerably in the rear of Pope. This he destroyed, and at the same time dispatched Stuart with his cavalry and infantry to Manassas Junction, seven miles nearer Washington. Here Stuart took a large amount of stores and many prisoners. Jackson had been ordered to throw his command between Washington and General Pope, and break up his railroad communication, and he did it to the letter.

While this bold manœuvre was in progress, Kearny and others of Heintzelman's Corps had, as we have said, arrived at Warrenton Junction and reported to Pope. The audacious movement of Jackson had placed himself and all Lee's army in great peril. Jackson was between the reënforcements advancing from Alexandria, and the main body of Pope. That General divined the opportunity, and immediately sought to cut off Jackson's retreat. On the morning of the 27th, he sent forward a column of 40,000, led by McDowell and Sigel, toward Gainesville, to prevent the advance of Longstreet and Lee through Thoroughfare Gap; and this force was to be supported by Reno and Kearny, who were directed upon Greenwich, thus meeting every avenue of approach by Longstreet and cutting off Jackson's road of retreat, while he and Hooker moved along the railroad toward Manassas Junction, there to encounter Jackson.

The plan was brilliant, and promised complete success. McDowell's main interposing column reached its assigned position, as ordered, on the night of the 27th. Hooker, moving toward Manassas Junction, met Ewell at Bristoe and drove him. *He* marched back and rejoined Jackson at Manassas Junction. And on the morning of August 28th it seemed as if Jackson could not escape. But at three A.M., he commenced his evacuation of Manassas, moving nearer Washington *via* Centreville, and seeking to make a detour around the forces encompassing him. Kearny, who was ordered forward toward Manassas, reached that point an hour after Jackson's rear-guard had left—but pushed forward, and late in the afternoon occupied Centreville, still behind the retreating Jackson, part of whose forces at six P.M. encountered King's division of McDowell's Corps, on the road toward Thoroughfare Gap, and a severe engagement ensued, in which the rebels had the advantage.

Pope, then at Centreville, heard of this collision at ten P.M. Sending orders to McDowell and King to hold their ground at all hazards, Kearny was pushed forward at one o'clock in the morning, from Centreville along the Warrenton turnpike, and ordered to hug Jackson close, so as to prevent his retreating northward toward Leesburg. This movement was rapidly executed; but other events soon made it abortive.

For, at three P.M. of the same day, August 28th, General Longstreet's advance reached Thoroughfare Gap, and passed through it; but encountering there a superior force, was checked and repulsed. Without delay, it was heavily reinforced. Our troops were outnumbered and driven. Early on the 29th, Longstreet's van was in Gainesville, passing on to the rescue of Jackson, and hastened by the roar of cannon; McDowell and King having gotten out of the way at night, retreating on Manassas Junction. Before noon, Longstreet came rapidly into action on the right of Jackson, already hotly engaged. The rebel army was once more reunited and felt itself invincible.

Acquainted with all the natural advantages of the country, Jackson disposed his troops, before Lee's advance had joined him, along the cut of an unfinished railroad, stretching from the Warrenton turnpike in the direction of Sudley's Mill, intended as part of the track to connect the Manassas road directly with Alexandria. The mass of his troops were sheltered in thick woods behind the railroad cut and the embankment, which formed a ready-made parapet. General Sigel attacked in the morning, and toward noon was joined by Reno, Hooker, and Kearny. There was brisk skirmishing all day. Longstreet, though Pope did not know it, had joined. There had been an artillery contest, of no great moment, all day. At three P.M., Hooker was ordered to attack. He, rather unwillingly, obeyed with great gallantry, but was at last driven back, and Kearny was ordered in likewise. Taking up his report, we find the following details: "In early afternoon General Pope's order was to send a pretty strong force directly to the front, to relieve the centre in the woods from pressure. Accordingly, I detached General Robinson with his brigade and other regiments, [enumerating them.] General Robinson drove forward for several hundred yards; but the centre of the main body being shortly after driven back and out of the woods, my detachments, thus exposed so considerably in front of all others, both flanks in air, were obliged to cease to advance and confine themselves to holding their own. At five o'clock, thinking, though at the risk of exposing my fighting line to enfilading, that I might drive the enemy by an unexpected attack through the woods, I brought up additional forces, and changed front to the left, to sweep with a rush the first line of the enemy. This was most successful. The enemy rolled up on his own right. It presaged a victory for us all. Still our force was too light. The enemy rapidly brought up heavy reserves, so that our further progress was impeded. General Stevens came up gallantly in action to support us, but did not have the numbers."

The report of the rebel General Hill tells this story thus: "The enemy prepared for a last and determined attempt. Their serried masses, overwhelming superiority of numbers, and bold bearing made the chances of victory to tremble in the balance. My own division had hardly one round per man remaining," etc. Says Early in his report: "My brigade and the Eighth Louisiana advanced through a field, and drove the enemy from the woods, and out of the railroad cut."

It is related that Kearny's success, so far as it went, was derived from an early knowledge of this ground. General Hooker knew nothing of this "cut," went in, and was driven away. Kearny's study of the country enabled him at once to understand the position. He advanced upon the enemy on both sides of the cut, while the others attacked it in front, and thus for a while, and until reënforcements came, he succeeded in driving the enemy..

The next day, August 30th, was the fatal second Manassas, far more destructive and injurious to the North than the disgraceful Bull Run, so long our stigma and dishonor. The forces of Pope were in sad condition. Defeated, disheartened, lacking food, and wearied with continual watching, fighting, and marching, thousands had straggled from their commands, and those that remained fought with little hope. The truth was, they lacked confidence in their commander. Their instinct was not very incorrect. They followed Mc-Clellan more readily than Pope; but even he had not fully their hearts. When he made up his mind to act, McClellan used his means more skillfully than Pope. He would probably have succeeded had he not been essentially and by nature a defensive general. Did he ever once attack? But such of the troops as were led by Kearny, Hooker, and Reno were ever ready—dispirited at last, indeed, but always ready when their generals led.

With this half-despairing army, Pope nevertheless determined again to fight the victorious rebels. Better perhaps to have retired upon McClellan, since he and his corps commanders seemed resolved not to advance to him. The disposition of the troops was as follows: Heintzelman, whose corps contained Hooker and Kearny, held the right of our line; McDowell the left, while Fitz-John Porter, Sigel, and Reno held the centre. By one of those accidents which sometimes occur in war, Lee and Pope had each determined to attack their adversary's left. So when Pope pushed forward for that purpose, he found no troops, and hence it was concluded that Lee was retreating up the Warrenton turnpike toward Gainesville. So, McDowell was ordered with three corps, Porter's in advance, to follow up the enemy and press him vigorously the whole day. But this provoked a heavy fire from the Confederate artillery, and, while the advance was checked, clouds of dust on the left showed that the enemy was moving to turn our extreme left. Immediately McDowell detached Reynolds from

Porter's left and directed him on a position south of the Warrenton turnpike so as to check this menace. This position was a hill called Bald Hill, situate west of another hill, on which the Henry house stands, between them being a brook or creek. While it was judicious in McDowell to occupy this point, the detachment of Reynolds for that purpose exposed the key-point of Porter's line. The enemy saw this, and poured in a destructive fire of artillery, and Porter's troops about five P.M. gave way and retired from the field. The Confederate line then advanced to cut off the retreat of the Union forces. Bald Hill was carried; it became doubtful whether even the "Henry House Hill" could be maintained so as to cover our retreat over Bull Run, for Longstreet had thrown around his right so as to menace that position. What I have said will enable us better to understand the further report of Kearny. "We took no part," he says, "in the fight of the morning, although we lost men by the enfilading fire of the enemy's batteries. A sudden and unaccountable evacuation of the field by the left and centre occurring about five P.M., on orders from General Pope, I massed my troops at the indicated point, but soon reoccupied, with Birney's Brigade, supported by Robinson, a very advanced block of woods. The key-point of this new line rested on the Brown house toward the creek. This was held by regiments of other brigades. Soon, however, themselves attacked, they ceded ground and retired without warning us. I maintained my position till ten P.M., when, in connection with General Reno and General Gibbon, assigned to the rear-guard, I retired my brigades. My command arrived at Centreville in good order at two o'clock this morning, and encamped in front of the Centreville forts. My loss in killed and wounded is over 750, about one in three; none taken prisoners except my engineer officer, who returned to the house supposed to be held by the troops alluded to."

Translated, this report shows the state of the case. It was Heintzelman—namely, Kearny and Hooker—who was to make the attack and open the battle. The enemy having massed to the other side of the line, they remained in position. When all was lost, Kearny remained and covered the retreat. He was ever in the post of danger, for he was always reliable and never to be defeated.

Arrived at Centreville, where were the corps of Franklin and Sumner, Pope remained there during all the 31st of August. And there Kearny penned the report from which I have quoted, the last he ever wrote. Thence, too, he wrote a letter in pencil, among the treasures of his family, a striking exhibition of his wonderful elasticity, his positive enjoyment of conflict. I am permitted to use this relic: "I wrote you yesterday morning; since then there has been a sort of Bull Run episode to the first day's fight. . . . It is dangerous work to fight in this army; you have to fight ten times your share, and expose yourself, to prevent the demoralizing effect of almost cowardice in others. Hooker's Division is almost the only exception. This army ran like sheep, all but a General Reno and a General Gibbon. As for myself, I was abandoned shamefully. My only salvation depended on holding a certain hill and house in the rear, adjoining me. In the darkness of twilight the enemy came, fired a few trifling shots, and Stevens's people ran, we alongside never dreaming of it. The worst was, General Heintzelman never informed me. I had a staff-officer taken prisoner, and I was only a few yards behind him. It was perfectly ridiculous; but he was so unsuspicious that I could not help him, as scouts were stealing in all around me. He was so surprised; it was very funny. I will tell you some other time. My regiments behaved like perfect loves—so beautifully steady. I staid for more than three hours after all the Americans but Reno and Stevens had left, and Reno was as much to the left as I was to the right, behaving very handsomely. My friend General Towers was wounded.

" This disaster is not Pope's fault, but rather Halleck's and McClellan's, high generals in places they are not fit for.

" It is tiresome to have one's victories ignored, as at Sangster's Station, and Williamsburg, and on the New-Market road, and to be confounded, though fighting hard and successfully, and exposing myself, as my nature unfortunately is, in other people's defeats. Yesterday would have been extremely amusing from its ridiculousness, if not so sad for our cause. Our men would not fight one bit; it was amusing to watch them. I foresaw it all three hours before it took place. But I am sorry for the cause."

Pope was comparatively safe at Centreville, but Lee had not quite given up the pursuit. The fullness of his victory was little understood by the Northern people. Indeed, till Grant, Meade, Sherman, and Sheridan taught us the way to victory, the strength of our arms lay in our ignorance. We did not know we were whipped; yet some did. And to them, little throughout the war can equal the horror of those fatal days of August and September, 1862. Nor was the cup of bitterness full till the fatal first of September took from the North the man upon whom all eyes were centering as *the* captain of the Army of the Potomac, the rejected, neglected, yet always ready, always victorious, Kearny.

On the 31st August, Jackson was again ordered forward, to turn our right, cut our communications, and intercept our retreat to Washington. A heavy storm on August 31st, and continuing September 1st, delayed his march. Kearny, the rear-guard of August 30th, with Reno and Stevens, was summoned again to the post of danger. He passed from front to rear like a triumphal conqueror. Regiment after regiment, as his erect and martial form appeared, hailed him with cheers upon cheers and followed his march with their shouts of admiration. The fighting men of each army met in this brief conflict—Jackson, Hill, and Ewell, with Reno, Stevens, and Kearny, the latter being this day assigned to the support of the others.   The action began at five P.M. near Chantilly.   General Stevens, of Reno's forces, led a charge, and was shot dead at the head of his troops.   Confused, and their ammunition being exhausted, they gave way.   "To repair this break," says the historian of the Army of the Potomac, "Kearny with the promptitude that marked him, sent forward Birney's Brigade, and presently, all aglow with zeal, brought forward a battery which he placed in position.   But there still remained a gap on Birney's right, caused by the retirement of Stevens's men.   This Birney pointed out to Kearny, and that gallant soldier, dashing forward to reconnoitre the ground, unwittingly rode into the enemy's lines and was killed.   In his death the army lost the living ideal of the soldier—a *preux chevalier*, in whom there was mixed the qualities of chivalry and gallantry as strong as ever beat beneath the mailed coat of an olden knight.   Like Desaix, whom Napoleon characterized as 'the man most worthy to be his lieutenant,' Kearny died offering a heroic breast to disaster."

The exact circumstances of his death demonstrate that he did not owe it to recklessness, (as generally supposed, and even directly asserted in Greeley's popular history of the war;) but to that provident care for his troops and professional zeal which were his marked characteristics.   The particulars were thus given by General Birney, his valued subordinate, afterward himself a martyr to his country's cause :   "During the battle of Chantilly my brigade was actively engaged.   I noticed that Stevens's Division had cowardly retreated, leaving a gap of half a mile on my right.   I asked General Kearny for Berry's Brigade to fill it; he stated that he had ordered the colonel commanding to report to me, and was indignant at his delay. But he said it was impossible that General Reno could have permitted *such* a Gap; that I must be mistaken; that there certainly were troops there of ours.   I assured him that there was not.   At this time it was raining, and the smoke from the batteries hung low. I galloped down to send in a regiment to my left.   He accompanied me, and as we leaped a ditch, his horse shied, and he remarked how disagreeable that a horse should behave so in a battle.   He then galloped to the right, and I saw him no more."   From Colonel, now General Medill, then his aid, I fill out the history.   General Kearny was on a black horse, and covered with his india-rubber cloak.   It was late in the evening—dark with clouds, the drizzly rain, and the shade of the woods.   He determined to see for himself if such a danger existed as such a gap in the Union line. Bidding Colonel Medill stay behind, he dashed forward to inspect. Pollard says: "General Kearny met his death in a singular manner. He was out reconnoitering, when he suddenly came upon a Georgia regiment. Perceiving danger, he shouted, 'Don't fire—I'm a friend'—but instantly wheeled his horse around, and, lying flat upon the animal, had escaped many bullets when one struck him at the bottom of the spine, and ranging upward, killed him almost instantly."

Private accounts, received since the war from Confederate sources, corroborate this account, differing only in unimportant particulars. General Kearny met his death, not from reckless or even careless exposure of his person; for the darkness, his dress, the color of his horse, the lateness of the hour, the place, and going alone, all rendered it unlikely that he should be observed; but the true cause was a sense of duty which impelled him personally to investigate an alleged necessity of changing the disposition of his largely outnumbered troops, and a generous disbelief that an officer so skillful as the almost equally lamented Reno could have overlooked a point and fact so critical.

And yet had he known, could he have suspected, in the midst of the neglect and want of justice with which he thought himself treated, how deeply he had graven his name upon the hearts of the people for whom he died, and how high he stood in the opinion of those in chief authority—nay! what a distinguished post might have been his had he lived even three days longer, that same sense of duty might have led him to an extreme of carefulness which would have prevented the sad catastrophe. At that very moment a letter was lying in the War Department, signed by the Assistant Secretary, ready for transmission, and which was forwarded after his death, of which the following is a copy:

"WAR DEPARTMENT, WASHINGTON CITY, }
September 1, 1862. }

"SIR: The Secretary of War directs me to acknowledge the receipt of your note of the 23d August, warmly urging that Major-General Kearny be assigned to one of the *corps d'armée* to be formed from the new levies. In reply, the Secretary instructs me to say that he knows no one more capable and worthy of command than Major-General Kearny, and that, on the reorganization of the army, he will endeavor to assign him a position commensurate with his eminent merits and distinguished services."

I have no warrant to state, and yet there is satisfactory ground for believing that even a higher position than that alluded to, namely, the command of the Army of the Potomac, would have been his, had he lived long enough to take Pope's place. Mr. Stanton had ceased to have respect for the ability of General McClellan. With that great man—but for whose strong will, instinctive justice, fearless patriotism, self-sacrificing assiduity, and wonderful executive ability the rebellion could never have been put down—halting and timorous hesitation and procrastination had no favor, while bravery, skill, and constant success like Kearny's had overcome original prejudice and detraction, and converted him into admiration and confidence. In a letter under his own hand to Mrs. Kearny he says: "His devoted patriotism, heroic courage, and distinguished military skill had secured to him the confidence and admiration of the Government, and endeared him to the people of the United States, who mourn his loss." And again: "His high appreciation by this department was shown by the rank he had won by long services and many gallant deeds, which would have been acknowledged by still higher command if he had not fallen upon the field of Chantilly." Nor should we omit to notice the generous conduct of General Lee in relation to his death. His body was immediately sent in. His horse, saddle, and sword were soon after returned; every effort was made, though unsuccessfully, to procure the property he carried upon his person; while deep sympathy was expressed for his untimely fall.

But language will vainly endeavor to describe the grief either of the army or the people at this sad event. Both had long been intelligent observers of his career—the army through daily opportunity, the people in spite of his contempt of newspaper fame and of the fulsome efforts made by so many officers or their friends to extol their merits while ignoring those of others. They knew him to be the saviour of the Army of the Potomac, and consequently of the country, on various occasions—at Williamsburg, by rushing on the field at the moment of almost complete defeat, after jamming his way for hours through miles of encumbering masses, and by his skill, rapidity, and personal exposure snatching splendid victory out of the very jaws of defeat; at Fair Oaks, by stopping the demoralized retreat of the divisions of Couch and Casey, withstanding the exultant rebels pressing on to the destruction of all the troops then on the Richmond side of the Chickahominy, until the arrival of Sumner restored the equality of numbers and enabled us to gain the victory of the next day; on the New-Market road, by again rushing in at the critical moment and beating back the triumphant masses of the pursuing rebels: they now saw him at the second Manassas, on the first day, checking the enemy after all others had tried without success, almost driving them back, and sustaining the unequal contest with their heavy reserves till night closed the combat; on the second day, standing till ten P.M. the rear-guard of our retreat, covering it, and at last himself retiring to take his place in camp in front of the advancing Confederates; and finally, at Chantilly, after passing from front to rear, losing his inestimable life in driving off the untiring Jackson from cutting our communications—a task which his lieutenant, Birney, whose whole experience in war had been under him, after his death performed, so that to Kearny's Division again was due the safety of the discomfited army. They saw elsewhere, from McClellan down, personal jealousies and personal views interfering with and restraining the energy of officers who should have known nothing but the duty and the enemy, while Kearny was always reliable, and, when danger was greatest, always there. And so they mourned for him, not with grief only, but with fear! For where, where was there then such another? Hooker had his bravery, but not his skill. Besides these two, what generals at that time, in that army, were famous, either for military skill or self-sacrifice? And the exulting rebels were more successful than ever! The North lay, to all appearance, at their mercy.

It is impossible to forget his funeral, or to refrain from recalling here its striking circumstances. Intended to be simple and quiet in the extreme, the people willed it to be an occasion of most solemn grief, and would not be restrained from the privilege of being mourners. Crowds daily thronged his mansion, while the dead hero lay awaiting burial, his bronzed features seeming to smile defiance even of the last conqueror. The city authorities of Newark almost compelled the procession to cross the Passaic and traverse the streets of the city, while deep bells tolled and wailing music thrilled the air. And, most affecting of all, from the entrance of the *cortége* into the city till it reached the point of departure from it, spontaneously, irrepressibly, in solemn silence, except for the tears and sobs of many, came forth a crowd of people, of all ages and each sex, reverently baring their heads in presence of the dead, for which they had stood hours in waiting, as orderly and as carefully placed as if under military directions, yet entirely unregulated by authority—an army of mourners, testifying thus the depth of their grief and their appreciation of their hero's services. On no occasion except the funeral of Lincoln was such regard, within my knowledge, manifested. And so he was borne to the venerable yard where his father and his dead darling boy lay; the magnificent service of its cathedral church was chanted over his remains, the final salute echoed through the great city, startling the speculations of its busy exchange. There he lies, not mouldering but embalmed while his memory is embalmed in the hearts of his countrymen.

The story of the military life of General Kearny embraces the history of the Army of the Potomac from its organization to the end of its second critical campaign; and, tedious as has been this review, it is yet but a sketch. The theme requires a volume. And then, aware that most have regarded him rather as a simple fighting man than a strategist and tactician—rather as an ambitious, restless soldier than a considerate, patient martyr; and holding him myself as distinguished for the highest qualities of heroism, I have thought the surest way of leading others to value him was to make abundant extracts from his correspondence, so that the real man as he lived and thought might rise and stand before us.

What are the essentials of the great soldier? Strategic skill, readiness and rapidity in tactical movements, the magnetic power to inspirit and control men, individually and in masses, personal bravery, coolness in excitement—these are the essentials to the great commander. Enthusiastic love of combat and military prescience added to the other qualities have been always the possession of those captains whom history hands down as men of genius. Add still to these a lofty sense of the soldier's duty, a love of country, and a chivalric readiness to sacrifice all for her, and the soldier becomes indeed a hero.

Have I not described Philip Kearny? His strategic views have been proved correct. What was the road to Richmond? Upon what line did the great general who, at the close of Kearny's career, was just rising above the horizon, fight out the dreadful contest? It was that line which Kearny always insisted was *the* line—the direct, straight path; driving the enemy before our columns; keeping the city of Washington and our supplies steadily defended by making each river we crossed a new road of connection with our base; leaving no room for flank movements by a force numerically inferior; keeping the foe throughout busily on the defensive; taking advantage of every mistake; increasing, if possible, every panic; allowing no rest or recuperation. Such a line necessitated vigorous and constant effort. Events have proved that its adoption concentrated the combat. We had no Jacksons after we initiated the simple policy of Grant.

Grant and Meade accomplished the great task after months of pertinacious fighting and flanking. How long would it have taken Kearny, leading 200,000 men on the same path and principles, to overwhelm the 40,000 who retreated hastily from Manassas, leaving behind them Quaker guns to illustrate McClellan's prudence?

The direct overland route had always an advantage. You knew its merits and demerits. There could be no novel engine of warfare introduced to scare or to overwhelm. The river route involved shipwreck, naval resistance, river obstructions. The Merrimac illustrated its difficulties, holding at bay, as she did, all our forces military and naval, till the strange Monitor, providential in the mode and time of her creation, and even more in the time of her arrival, saved, with her fifty men and her revolving turret, our vast army from powerlessness or ruin.

As a tactician, General Kearny had no superior. He was always at home, knowing exactly what to do and how to do it. His facility of organization was remarkable. His camp was a marvel, so orderly, so clean, so carefully regulated. There was not a rule of drill with which he was not familiar. There was no end to the perfection at which he aimed; and marvelous were the results of his discipline. The First New-Jersey Brigade were acknowledged to be among the best troops in the army; they were only what their general made them. But the best illustration of his skill in tactics, and his power over men, is found in the battle of Williamsburg. His division had only known him three days, yet he handled them so confidently, so coolly, so judiciously, that they leaped at once, new and raw troops though they were, to the rank of the fighting division of the army. And, throughout all the battles he fought, his tact in command was conspicuous. At Manassas, with his *échelon* movement on the enemy; at Fair Oaks, where, dexterously changing front, he established a new line, and, seizing his opportunity, found safety in the moment defeat and capture stared him in the face; at the New-Market road; in fact, at every battle; he managed his division with a simple ease and readiness which demonstrated his fitness for the highest command.

But it was his magnetic power to inspirit and command which was his chief distinction, the result, doubtless, of the conjunction in him of great personal bravery, coolness in action, promptness of resolution, strength of will, thorough knowledge of human nature, and of that evident enthusiasm, called by the French, *élan*, which lifted him up in a sort of military intoxication, and made all follow him as they follow one inspired. Considering these qualities *seriatim*, his personal bravery was simply amazing. When Scott called him "bravest of the brave," he spoke but the literal truth. He absolutely knew no fear. Like most soldiers, he approached fatalism in sentiment. His time was to come—when, who knew? Who could hasten, who defer it? Riding up and down, in front of his troops at Williamsburg, he shouted to the rebels, within pistol-shot, "Shoot away!" while to his troops, securely posted among the timber, he cried, "Boys, don't be afraid; they're not shooting at you, they're shooting at *me*. Give it to them!" We can almost imagine his martial form before us, erect as a statue, appearing to be part of his restless, bounding horse, all the soldier in his looks, his eye fired with the excitement of the strife he loved, his single arm raised aloft, at one moment in defiance to his foes, at the other, encouraging his inexperienced and timid troops—the impersonation of enthusiastic war; while his voice, trumpet-toned, shouted alternately cool command and

proud derision. No wonder that he seemed to the rebel hordes the
"one-armed devil." No wonder that, for very shame, the craven among
our own people were craven no longer, and men he never saw before
followed him as if some grim denizen of another world, suddenly
sent to lead to victory. Undoubtedly his unrivaled martial bearing
was a great, perhaps the chief, source of his personal influence. But
his success was much more due to his peculiar coolness in action. An
associate in Mexico described him as even then growing cooler as the
battle raged. This is not unusual with impulsive temperaments.
Where the nervous system is strong, men tremble before danger or
exertion, and cool as it is realized and met. It is so with all great
orators. It is so, we believe, with great soldiers also. In both cases,
it is a seeming inspiration to the actor as well as the observer.

Looking deeper still, we think his power over his troops was the
result of a natural love of combat—not at all a rare quality; developed, often, in forensic strife—oftener yet in those severer contests
which war occasions, and increased by professional study and ambition. And Philip Kearny was in love with his profession, a thorough student of the art of war. His military library was of the
highest character; and not only in youth and leisure, but in the march-
ings, and amid the toils of his life in actual service, he was a severe
student. By nature sleepless and nervous, he spent the nights, till
early morning, habitually in study. The campaigns of Napoleon, of
Frederick, of Marlborough, were his familiar themes of thought, and,
if need were, conversation. He was ready, at any moment, to adopt
their most accomplished schemes.

And so he had a confidence in himself, so full of simplicity and
so approved by success, that none could charge him with conceit or
hardihood. He did not thrust it upon strangers, but to his intimates
he expressed it without thought of reticence. No one cared less to
appear what he was not. He scorned it. But when sure that he possessed a quality, or had won a distinction, he made his claim as for
justice. No word that ever fell from him indicated that he looked to
the possibility of his commanding the army; yet to his wife he wrote:
"I feel that I could handle this large army as easily as I did my Jersey brigade." And he was not mistaken. Why not? There was
not a man in all our army who had had equal experience. He had
been beside Scott from Vera Cruz to Mexico, his body-guard, acquainted, or having every opportunity of seeing and understanding
all his plans. He had besides fought in Algeria, and, in the campaign
of Italy, had aided in the movement and control of the largest armies
the world ever beheld. He had studied his profession, not as a duty
or for a livelihood, but from the love of it, with a zeal which never
flagged and with opportunities unrivaled. All that he was, he looked

and acted, and hence his power over individuals and the masses. Add to this his intimate knowledge of human nature, belonging to him through his opportunities as a man of the world, increased by his sympathy with humanity, (and never did more generous heart beat in human bosom;) and you see why it was that Philip Kearny was adored by the army, by his officers, by the country—that *his* cross is the American cross of honor—that his name is cherished by the survivors of his command as Frenchmen cherish that of Napoleon.

Those who have appreciated his correspondence can not fail to have noted his extraordinary military prescience. "Let McClellan go to Harper's Ferry," he said, "and Manassas will be evacuated." And so it was. "If McClellan approach Richmond by the way of the river, there will be nothing but delay and disaster; it will uncover Washington, and we shall be degraded abroad and defeated at home." And so it was. "We shall not be able to pass Yorktown." Nor did we. "Such arrangements around Richmond will create disaster—in a few hours we shall suffer." Sooner than anticipated the struggle came. "We shall be cut off, but I shall escape." And it was even so. "What next, but either inexplicable evacuation or an attack upon, and severance of, our communications?" And hardly were the words written before they were fulfilled. "Change of base is but a phrase; we must run out like rats." And it was so. This intuitive perception of what was to be seems extraordinary. It indicates Napoleonic qualities. And yet it was the result of industrious application. General Kearny was in love with the profession of arms. He lived in it alone. Our leading officers took it as a trade, and lived by the study and practice of its *peaceable* or defensive arts. He studied but one branch of it, fighting, and that as a profession. He was fitter, really, to lead the army in the beginning than any other man except Scott—and he grew in competency as the war went on.

Shall I not press further in my eulogy? Had he not the hero's sense of duty—the patriot's love of country? It is thus he writes home in August, 1862: "I am distressed to think of your anxiety as to me: dismiss it. In battle some fall so soon and others escape so miraculously that it must be left to God's will. I certainly know the exposures of war, but have been spared so mercifully (not but that I am ready in all peril) that my heart is softened; and I feel that it would be wickedness not to be sensible of Divine protection. I have in danger such an instinctive scorn of the enemy and indifference, that I truly have seen, with little or no emotion, that I was often the 'observed of all observers.' Still, as long as I am here to devote myself to the war, no risk ever comes up to the sad thought ever on my mind of separation from you and home." This is not the defiant soldier, the reckless lover of contest, the ambitious officer " seeking the bubble reputation, even in the cannon's mouth." It is his soliloquy, this written without a thought of its reaching any eye but that of his other self; it explains and illustrates his bravery—part constitutional, part the result of a deep conviction that he was in the path of duty, and was to live or die according to His will who sustains alike the universe and the sparrow! And then his patriotism. Most of those conspicuous in this war were lifted up from obscurity, or comparative discomfort in life to the stations they occupied. Patriotism, pure and simple, abounded far more in the ranks than among the officers. There, it flourished abundantly indeed. But those who first received appointments as superior officers seldom failed to better their worldly position. Not so with Kearny. What did he need? what did he not leave? A princely fortune, the luxury and the *salons* of Paris, all the gratifications which money could bestow, the affinities of social life—for his American friends were almost to a man Southerners—the delights of home, for the camp and its hardships, the wild excitement and perpetual dangers of the field. He left them for no holiday soldiering, no ambitious self-aggrandizement, but to be present where bullets flew thickest and shells fell fastest; to dare, to lead, to insure death unless miraculously guarded. Hear again how he writes in July, 1862: "As to their not appreciating me, be sure that they do so, most fully—rather too fully. It causes them always to select me and my division for every thing that is dangerous, or likely to go wrong. It makes very little odds. I am sure that as a high-toned gentleman I do not serve from petty ambition. I am too truly disinterested to make a civil war a source of *éclat*. I have far too sincere an affection for the Southerners, whose course I disavow, yet love as old associates, to care to aggrandize myself in their misery and hopeless struggles. Mismanagement or treachery may restrain the efforts of the North for a season, but its triumph must come; and all whom I have been brought up with in childhood and cultivated in manhood must be swept away—their families impoverished, and themselves a by-word. I am sorry to see this army saddled with imbeciles; and for myself, I know that I must rise; still I would be stifled at the thought that this world's ambition could repay me the absence from you and the sad, sad changes since leaving our cherished friends in France." Think of his course when his friends were annoyed and baffled in the effort to secure his appointment; when among the congressional delegation of New-Jersey, *but one* could be found earnestly to recommend him; when, with all his capacity and reputation, he needed political influence to procure for him the post of brigadier. And when Bull Run came upon us, that terrible disclosure of inefficient generals and discipline, immediately he announced his readiness to go in any post—to lead a regiment or serve in one. His maimed body debarred him from the ranks. But wherever he could serve, he was ready to serve. He was the patriot personified, and from the noblest motives. Nationality was his great argument. "What are we, unless Americans?" was his controlling thought. And when the war was raging, long ere the proclamation of freedom, how directly does he settle the duty of the North to the slave; how simple, how clear his view! In his sketch, already quoted, as to how the slaves should be disciplined, he says: "This idea of black adjuncts to the military awakens nothing inhuman. It but prevents the slave, run away or abandoned to us, from becoming a moneyed pressure upon us. It eventually would prepare them for freedom—*for surely we do not intend to give them up to their rebel masters.*" Nationality for America—freedom for the slave, these his simple direct intellect descried to be the issues of the contest; and so, in an instant, the natural aristocrat became the Union Republican! Not to talk only—not as a politician, but as a patriot to fight and die for these significant issues!

The world is full of the praise of Jackson. Monuments rise from the impoverished South to his memory. Their little ones are taught to worship him as the incarnation of patriotic military genius. And he *was* a genius; and if you can call treason earnestly believed in, treason which forgot Washington, and Madison, and Pinckney of South-Carolina, and Marshall, and crowds of other national Virginians and Southerners, and aimed at destroying the nation they formed; if you can call that patriotism; if you can think him a noble Christian and man of honor who, educated by the nation, and time and time again solemnly sworn to maintain and defend the nation, never once his State, drew the sword she had given him, devoted the talents she had nurtured for her destruction—then *he* was a patriot! But is the misguided Jackson to be canonized, and Kearny forgotten? Both served for an idea, not for self-aggrandizement. The one was controlled by half fanatic piety—piety which, among Southerners and Southern sympathizers, in John Brown was contemptible and but aggravated treason, but which in Jackson almost deifies. The other by a simple sense of the duty of a gentleman to his country which, concealed under outward carelessness, his letters show was humble and full of faith in Divine power. Sentiment impelled each to self-forgetfulness; to the perpetual hazard of life; finally, to the suffering of death for the cause he had espoused. In military skill, they closely resembled each other. Enterprise, energy, prompt and rapid execution, quickness and fertility of design, magnetic power over men—the highest military skill and efficiency distinguished both, and gave both constant success. The necessities of the South, the wisdom and concentration of purpose of Lee, gave Jackson scope. The absence of such qualities in our Commander-in-Chief retained Kearny in comparative obscurity

—obscurity from which he rose at last like a star to the zenith, hardly before the fatal moment of his sinking in dissolution. And yet he lived long enough to be the idol of his men, the admiration of all the army—to win the regard of his country for all time. Let traitors honor the traitor whose misguided conscientiousness helps make their cause respectable. Let patriots mourn over the early grave of Kearny, whose love of country drew his sword, and who, after a career abounding in chivalric heroism and military success, died martyr for law, freedom, and the nation.

I could wish, ere I close, to paint the man, not as the world knew him, but as those did whose fortune it was to see his inner self; to delineate him justly, with all the lights and shades, the good and evil, joined in peculiar contradiction, which made up his character; to suggest the causes which moulded his mental and moral organization. It would be a picture of a strong but unusually impulsive nature, victim of circumstances and of misdirection, bereft in early life of the sweet influences of maternity, fostered into worldliness which it despised yet thought itself compelled to adopt, excitable alike for good and evil, distinguished for *abandon* whether as saint or sinner—a character which, religiously directed, would have made him, if need were, the Christian martyr; which, being directed irreligiously, led him far away from good, yet with an under-current constantly drawing him to better things. Outrageously violent, he was speedily cooled, and then absolutely unjust in self-abasement and apology. Fierce as the lion in combat, he was tenderness personified toward those whom he loved. Hear Philip Kearny utter such words as these: "Your letters are so sad, to me ever oppressed with sadness when I come back to my own sorrows and your same sorrows, to trace your accounts so varying of our lost loved precious boy. But as a protector to you, how little do I care to live longer! It is true that in danger I do not think of it one way or the other, danger has been so much a habit to me. But when I drop my professional duties and turn my thoughts to you and home, how sadly I am oppressed! Our dear angel boy, whom God gave us but to take away. His first smile, his last look! God knows how much I suffer, and you how much more. God give us strength!" And then his justice was remarkable. He has paid tradesmen for their trouble in twice presenting their bills. He would keep his word about a debt, if he rode at night to pay. He hated shams, and cowardice, physical and moral. He demanded of all their duty—that done, he was exaggerated in generosity. Strange man indeed! It is impossible to reconcile his moral inconsistencies. Yet, as the hour of his death approached, he seemed to alter. The day before he was killed, he conversed long and seriously with an earnest chaplain on the theme of personal re-

ligion. The death of his son had evidently impressed him. As plainly
did it appear for days before his death that he had a presentiment of
it. The loss of the scabbard of his sword had seemed to him an ill
omen. He was solicitous that his staff should be near him, a thing
marked as unusual. Who can speak for his emotional being? The
grace of God flies faster than the bullet!

Why did Kearny die? Why did Mitchel, and Reno, and Stevens, and Wadsworth, and Sedgwick, and Bayard, and hosts of others
especially distinguished for capacity and patriotism—perish? why did
so many, many thousand men of lesser fame? Why was the North
so long unable to detect real merit, and insanely led to glorify and
almost worship mediocrity or timidity? why so long waste of our
tremendous power? why did it take five years of combat to quell this
rebellion, when, had such as Kearny led, the 200,000 men who lay
around Washington in 1861 might have swept the rebel army, now
known to have been really weakened by their victory at Bull Run, out
of existence? Why all our sufferings, all our sorrows, our present debt
and the impoverishment of the rich and happy South—why? Do we
not know? With the past under our eye, do we not comprehend? It
was to bring this whole people to understand and appreciate the
enormity of that great wrong which our Constitution, blessed struc-
ture that it is, nevertheless defended and perpetuated. It was to
compel the great North to cast into the sea this cause of all our
misery. It was to teach us that God reigns, that he is of purer eyes
than to behold iniquity, that he hath made all men of one blood. It
was to compel us to eradicate our prejudices and to believe, really,
that he has created all men equal, and that upon us it devolved to
insure their equality before the law. It was to persuade us to ex-
tirpate that cancer—slavery; to cut it out *from its roots*, so that this
republic might be no *sham*, but in very truth a form of government
which acknowledges all men to be created equal! Let us obey the
divine monition. Let us establish this land as a place where all *men*
can rule who are fitted to rule; where, if possible, none shall share in
ruling who are unfitted; and thus let us insure to all time the perpetu-
ation of that republic whose life has been bought with so much blood
and suffering.